# HOW L...
# HIS TONGUE

# A
# SAGA OF SOULS STORY

## Derek Nelsen

Summit Pen

Copyright© 2021 by Derek Nelsen
All rights reserved.

This is a work of fiction. Names, characters, businesses, places, events, locales, and incidents are either the products of the author's imagination or used in a fictitious manner. Any resemblance to actual persons, living or dead, or actual events is purely coincidental.

No part of this book may be reproduced in any form or by any electronic or mechanical means, including information storage and retrieval systems, without written permission from the author, except for the use of brief quotations in a book review.

Edited by Amanda Ashby
Copy Edited by Will Clifton
Cover Design by betibup33

Published by Summit Pen
eBook ISBN: 978-1-7351240-2-5
Paperback ISBN: 978-1-7351240-3-2

My mother taught me the importance of writing thank you notes.

Mom, this book is for you.

Thank you for your faith, in God and in me.
For loving me when I was unloveable.
For believing in me when I doubted myself.
For supporting me when I couldn't.
And most of all, for your example.

...and for chess, and roller coasters, and terrifically crooked Monopoly games.

# CONTENTS

| | | |
|---|---|---|
| 1 | Poor Allies | 1 |
| 2 | A Queen's Cruelty | 9 |
| 3 | Back to the Ships | 13 |
| 4 | Meeting Ubbi | 17 |
| 5 | Scone | 24 |
| 6 | Churches, Skirts and Empty Streets | 29 |
| 7 | The Sheriff's Son | 34 |
| 8 | The Stone of David | 39 |
| 9 | Pyre in the Square | 44 |
| 10 | Lost Boys | 50 |
| 11 | Pride and Alcohol | 53 |
| 12 | Last Words | 57 |
| 13 | Ships, Axes, Hammers and Swords | 62 |
| 14 | Vengeance of a Disgraced Son | 69 |
| 15 | Real Warriors Lead | 72 |

| | | |
|---|---|---|
| 16 | The First Sheriffson Raid | *78* |
| 17 | Delivering the Stone | *83* |
| 18 | Key to the Kingdom | *91* |
| 19 | Crossing Into Fae | *95* |
| 20 | Tricks of the Raid | *101* |
| 21 | Uncatchable | *105* |
| 22 | Pledge to the Jarl | *108* |
| 23 | The Stone and the Soul | *113* |
| 24 | The Returning | *122* |
| 25 | Have You Read Viking Lost? | *125* |
| 26 | About the Author | *127* |

# POOR ALLIES

"I still think this is a bad idea." Tor ran the whetstone along Ice Breaker's edge. He always sharpened his sword when speaking of war. It helped him focus. "Who cares about Ketill Flatnose anyway? We're doing fine."

Olaf crouched down to look Tor in the eye. He liked to rub it in that no matter how tall Tor was compared to everyone else, he was bigger. So were trolls, Tor often reminded him.

"Nobody cares about old Flatnose, but Harald Fairhair cares about the Southern Isles — so we care about the Southern Isles." Olaf had said it to the men so many times Tor wondered if he could gather his thoughts without repeating it. Power was how Olaf got things done, not words.

"Not all of us," Tor countered. Olaf stood and looked down at him.

"We've been trading nicely with these stinkin' Picts all spring to earn an audience with their king, and you won't be talking me out of seeing him. Now grow some stones and tell Wid we're ready to meet King Drest before he gets himself murdered like the last leader of the Picts. The way these people go through kings we may never get a chance like this again." Olaf pinned Tor's blade against the sharpening stone. "And remember, if the Picts think I'm a Jarl, then I'm a Jarl. Don't be so proud."

"Pictish traders don't bestow titles." Tor sheathed his sword. "Remember that."

"Maybe they're seeing something we're not."

Tor turned back. "What are you getting at, Olaf?"

"You and I have built something here. We are negotiating with kings—kings! We are partners—brothers, even. And that will never change. But men of power want to negotiate with someone on their level. You know this is true." Olaf shrugged his huge shoulders. "Can I help it if they always assume that the big man's in charge?"

"If the Pict assumes you're a Jarl or a Sea King or Odin himself, then fine, I'll play along, but don't let it go to your head."

"Without a leader, we will never be seen as equals to these men." Olaf put his massive hand on Tor's shoulder. "Let's settle this now. I'll be Jarl and you be my General. How's that sound? When I gain power, you gain power."

Tor answered with a grunt. He hated Olaf for pushing this again. What happened to raiding until they'd gotten their glory? And silver enough to get some land and slaves to farm it? If Olaf could speak Pictish, Tor would've probably stayed home for this one.

"Since when did we want power, or position?"

Olaf furrowed his brow and cast down a hard look. "Don't make me challenge you for it in front of the Pict."

"Maybe we should settle this now." Tor strangled Ice Breaker's hilt and put his chin up to Olaf's chest, his eyes burning holes in the would-be Jarl. Olaf was a beast, big as a polar bear, but Tor wasn't afraid. Probably the only man who wasn't. He and Olaf had tangled many times since they first met as boys, and there were no losers between them.

Olaf's scowl gave way to a gap-toothed grin. "Calm down, my friend. I don't want to fight. Just trying to get you to start thinking practically." He wrapped his enormous arms around Tor, picked him up off his feet as only Olaf could, and nearly crushed the air out of his lungs. "Now, come on, let's sell our souls to a Pict king."

# HOW UBBI LOST HIS TONGUE

Tor never liked that saying. He only had one soul, and he intended to keep it.

It was early, and the fog rolling out from the Pictish moors was so dense that Tor couldn't tell sea from shore. As they made their way through pre-dawn camp, smoke from twenty smoldering fires added to the blur. Tor kicked Hallstein as he passed, one of ninety men still sleeping off the previous night's drunk.

He never knew where Einar and Hallstein found their blood weed, but somewhere between the Southern Isles and Pictavia they'd gotten enough to brew a strong batch of firewater.

Olaf was still teetering from celebrating the alliance they were on their way to make. But he'd sober by the time it mattered.

"Too much drink last night?" Tor asked.

"I'll be fine before the sun comes up." Olaf took a drink from a skin before tucking it back inside his coat.

"You'd better be. If you're going to play the politician, then you'll need to do it with a smile."

"Ubbi!" Tor woke the boy from a dead sleep. "If you want to raid, you've got to prove yourself worthy first."

"I'm awake." Ubbi jumped to attention. "Just resting my eyes. The ponies are fed and watered—just got to hitch them to the cart." Ubbi rubbed his eyes as he searched. "Njáll! Ve! Hitch those Ponies to the cart for Tor and Olaf."

'These boys can't even guard the horses, Tor." Olaf jerked Ubbi off his feet. "What if some Pictish ghoul had come out of them woods to steal those horses, eh?" The boy looked like he might piss himself. "I ought to tie your hands to an oar for a couple of days for dozing off like that. And you want to go on a raid." Olaf shoved Ubbi to the ground. "Now get me a horse."

Tor hated that Olaf never invested in the boys. Someday they'd be depending on them on the battlefield, and making them ready came from training and trusting them with responsibility. Not filling their heads with derision.

Olaf mounted a pony, and Tor joined Wid, their Pict guide, in the cart. It was time to leave the safety of the ships and crew and strike an alliance with the Pict King, Drest.

During the hours of riding, the only entertainment was Olaf's cursing as his feet dipped in and out of the cold and fetid water of the moors. Ubbi had given him the largest pony, but it was still too short for Olaf. Served him right for wanting to ride in the first place. He should've put Wid the little Pict on the pony and joined Tor on the cart. But that would be too humbling for a would-be Jarl.

When the village came into sight, Tor reminded their guide of their arrangement.

"Wid..." He thought of the right way to say what he wanted in the Pictish tongue. *Ah, yes.* He ground his teeth. "Our crew will burn your village to the ground if we aren't back at the ships before sunset."

Wid's eyes swelled, then he nodded slowly. Their guide was a short, fat Pict. The only fat one Tor had ever seen. His perpetually bad breath whistled a little when it passed through his broken front tooth whenever he smiled. Smiling was another unPictlike thing he liked to do.

Wid dismounted with some effort. His blue and gray checkered sash was held to with a beautiful gold brooch, one Tor had removed from the cloak of a dead Irish Priest. He'd planned to bring it back to his mother if he ever made it home again, but when he showed it to Wid, to prove they had a common enemy in the Angles, the wry little imp mistook it for a gift. Olaf insisted it was a small price to pay. "Maybe after all this is over, you'll find him with a spear in his chest. Then you can have it back. But let's get his King's army first."

"Traders are a special kind of slimy. No matter where I go, they're cleanest on the outside, and dirtiest on the in."

## HOW UBBI LOST HIS TONGUE

The path merged with another, and another again, until they were on a worn, grassless road leading them through the bogs to an archway of twisted trees. Four guards were waiting. Their faces were smeared with blue paint that smelled of woad and horse piss. All Picts, except Wid the trader, smelled like that. But when the wind shifted and raised their Pictish skirts, a sour tinge of sweat added a new foulness to the air.

"No matter what," Tor feigned a smile as he warned Olaf in the Norse tongue, "pretend Drest's hall smells as fresh as the open sea."

He could see Olaf struggling to keep from shaking his head as another skirted man led them to a hall as uninspiring on the outside as Olaf's father's barn, except for the blue on the painted door.

Why had Tor let Olaf talk him into this?

For a moment they stood in the open door. The packed hall needed twice as many candles to claim it was ill lit. Now Tor knew why Picts were so small and skinny. Even their King was poor.

The place reeked of sheep, sweat, and beer. In that order. Tor's eyes were slow adjusting to the dark. There were at least two hundred dirty, blue-streaked faces cackling in the Pictish tongue like a room full of chickens. The room was so packed it reminded him of the time they lost one of their ships to a storm and spent an entire day rowing home with men piled on top of each other's laps.

As they stepped in, hundreds of mugs hit the tables. Then silence, as mouths shut and heads turned. Eyes squinted as if they hadn't seen the sun that day.

"*Uff da!*" A lightning bolt of pain shuddered down Tor's spine as he cracked his head on the blue doorway. He scowled at Olaf for laughing. *Oaf.*

A wild-haired, middle-aged Pict shook a portly, plain woman off his arm and forced her to take her seat at a table on the far side of the hall. She was well-dressed and clean and fit in about as much as Tor and Olaf.

The wild-haired Pict leaned on his cane and slowly limped their way.

"These are the Northmen?" he asked Wid in the Pictish tongue.

"This is Jarl Olaf," Wid replied, neglecting to introduce Tor.

The wild one took Olaf by the arm and led him away.

Tor flushed with anger. He took a deep breath, exhaled slowly, and pushed Wid aside on his way to catch up. "I am Tor, Olaf's general and interpreter."

Olaf elbowed Tor, and Tor interpreted back in Norse.

"The wild one with the cane wants to escort you to the foot of the throne where you can grovel for the king's favor like a dog begging for scraps," Tor said.

"I don't grovel."

"Ah, but as your mouthpiece, I'll make sure you do." Tor couldn't help but laugh as Olaf struggled to hide his anger behind a false smile. "That's a good politician."

The tables were full of plaid sashes. Wide eyes and sneers followed as the wiry man led them toward an empty, elevated throne.

Tor looked back at Wid for guidance, but two guards had held him at the door. He shrugged and offered a useless nod of support.

When Tor and Olaf had considered making this alliance, they knew this would be the riskiest part of the plan. For men like them, warfare wasn't nearly as intimidating as diplomacy.

Along with pitchers and cups of ale, axes and short swords littered the tabletops. The farther the wild one hobbled them away from the door, the more it occurred to Tor that, although he couldn't tell the blue-faced Picts apart, a pair like him and Olaf would be hard for any of them to forget. If just one of them were recognized from any number of raids they'd made on Pictavia's shores, they'd be raising their drinking horns in Valhalla tonight. Olaf seemed calm enough, but Tor's heart was pounding like it was trying to kick down a church door.

They stopped in front of the empty throne.

The man hobbled a circle around Tor and Olaf. He poked Olaf in the stomach. Tor watched Olaf's response, thinking the plan could end right there because of a crazy Pict with a cane. But to Olaf's credit, he only snarled, like a big wolf stuck in a cage of his own ambition.

"Ask him how long 'til the King arrives," Olaf growled. "I don't like the smell of these people."

A skinny, freckled, fawn-headed boy sitting across from the clingy brunette spat his drink onto the floor and almost choked to catch his breath.

"Ow!" the boy yelped when the wild man cracked him in the shin with his cane. Then he rapped Tor on the foot to regain his attention.

*Patience.* Tor inhaled slowly.

"You Northmen have terrorized us for many years. Have you two ever visited our lands before?"

"Only to trade." Tor struggled to keep from taking the man's cane and beating him with it. "I believe you're thinking of the Danes. We saw some of their ships heading out to sea as we came down the coast."

"What'd he say?" Olaf nudged Tor with his elbow.

The boy looked like he was listening. Tor cocked up his head and spoke to Olaf through smiling teeth. "He's asking where we are from. Let me handle this." This wasn't the first time Tor was glad Olaf only spoke Norse.

"Can we be honest with each other?" The old cripple poked at Tor's sword. "I am not a fool—like the trader, Wid, who only thinks of profit. Do you think he's convinced me to give you my army? I know you only have three ships and less than ninety men. I have thousands."

Tor swallowed, finally recognizing who was speaking to them. Not a cripple, but a king.

"You Northmen all look the same to me." He raised an eyebrow to an attractive blond sitting next to the boy, then flipped Tor's hair with his cane. "But I didn't need the trader's introduction to see that you're not Harald Fairhair. And he's not Ketill Flatnose." He swung the cane up toward Olaf's face, but Olaf caught it with his big mitt.

The entire hall dropped their cups and snatched up their weapons.

"Let go of the cane, Olaf," Tor said in as calm a voice as he could. "This is King Drest. Or hadn't you guessed?"

"Well, remind him I'm a Jarl, then." Olaf threw the end of the cane down toward the King's feet.

Drest laughed. Uneasily, the hall started laughing with him. "Sit. I'm sure you'll be able to stop the giant if he tries to take my stick." The Picts laughed, but the room remained tense.

Olaf's face reddened.

"Stay calm, Olaf," Tor said. "If that's as bad as it gets, then we might make it out of here yet."

"Father?" the skinny boy got up from his seat next to the pretty blond who was clearly his mother.

The plain brown-haired woman sitting across from the boy tried to stop him, but he wriggled by untouched. That one was likely the queen.

The King rolled his eyes and waved him up. After the boy whispered something in his ear, the King looked hard up to Olaf, frowned, and dismissed the boy back to his seat. The boy gave Tor an uneasy look as he passed.

# A QUEEN'S CRUELTY

"Well, my friends," said the king, "I need you to do me a favor before I can trust you with my army. I mean, I can't risk sending Pict warriors north to follow you, whoever you are, into Ketill Flatnose's territory to start a war with the Angles without some proof of your allegiance, can I?"

If Tor had translated that for Olaf, the King's head would've ended up on his stick.

"What did you have in mind?" Tor glanced down at the boy who was listening a little too intently for his taste. Tor and Olaf met eyes.

"I have a favor to ask."

Tor turned to stare at Wid, and by the look on his face he knew he was about to lose something more valuable than another gold brooch. *Thieving Picts.*

"There's a local sheriff that refuses to pay his tribute. Nothing too much for your crew to handle. Some of my men are from his village, and I don't need them wondering which side of the fight they're on if it comes to that. You understand." King Drest leaned forward on his throne. Quietly, he whispered, "Bring them in line, and we'll rid the Northern Isles of the Gaels, together."

"You want us to collect your taxes?" Tor knew with Picts there was always a catch. It was the reason he hadn't wanted to make a deal with these devils in the first place.

"Well, yes. That too. But mostly I need you to get proof of their allegiance to me. I can't afford a fractured kingdom if I plan to ally with Northmen to attack the Angles." King

Drest leaned back in his throne and scratched the sparse, wiry hair on his pointy chin.

Tor wondered what the last Pict King did to earn the dagger he got in his back. "Exactly how are we supposed to get proof of their allegiance?"

"Deirfiúr!" Drest called a name Tor couldn't make out. Some of those Pictish names were hard to get, even without the accent. A witch, dressed all in black, stepped out of the shadows. Even her hair was covered. The crone sidled up beside the throne, and they whispered back and forth. The room fell dead silent, but Tor still couldn't make out any of what they were saying. He thought Drest might have called her his sister, once.

Olaf leaned in, "What's going on?"

Tor looked at the boy and leaned in close to Olaf and whispered, "They want us to run an errand for them. I don't like it."

"We need this—"

"Hush." Tor clapped his fingers to his thumb up near Olaf's face. "I think that boy is a spy."

"But we're in their court." Olaf peered over in time to see the boy look away.

"See? I think he understands. Look at his mother. She's Norse, ja?"

"Forget the boy. Errands for Drest gets us an army, while errands for Flatnose gets us nothing." Olaf crossed his arms. "Agree to anything. I can't stand being in Flatnose's shadow."

"That's good." Drest waved the woman off, leaned forward on his cane, and addressed Olaf directly, as if he could understand. "Bring back the keystone. They would never give it up except for fealty or death. Either is okay with me."

"What is the keystone?" Tor asked.

"Just an ancient trinket. You Northmen wouldn't see the value in it, but it's something my people revere." The

## HOW UBBI LOST HIS TONGUE

king cast a shifty smile to the witch.
Tor did not trust that look. Olaf recognized it as well, but nudged Tor with his elbow. Olaf's ambition always overshadowed his good sense.
"We will try to avoid bloodshed." Tor exhaled, defeated.
"Of course." Drest smiled, exposing a mouthful of tobacco-brown broken stumps. The king's teeth were worse than Wid's. "This is a political task, not a military one."
"Maybe, King Drest, you should send a representative, too—so your sheriff understands our aims as well." To be a witness or an instigator, Tor didn't care, as long as a Northman wasn't blamed for drawing first blood.
The portly queen stood, staring bitterly at the blond across the table. "Send Orri."
The blond woman's face crumped. She wrapped her arms around the boy and vigorously shook her head.
The King's look cast a shadow over the queen.
The boy shook his mother off. "I can do it, Father."
Father. Tor couldn't help but smile. The king's bastard mocks his queen.
"All right." Drest looked almost proud, as if he'd never been impressed by his son before.
The boy turned pale but straightened his back. Somewhere between panic-stricken and proud.
Tor gave the King a false smile. What kind of man would send his own young son off with foreigners he didn't even trust with his own army? "And will you be sending anyone else?" *Perhaps you'd like to get rid of the queen while you're at it?*
"You will find him very capable." Drest watched his son stand taller still.
"He's no Viking, but his mother is your kind," the Queen said in a malicious voice. "I think this will be good for him. He's much too coddled for a Pict." The queen cast

a stern glance at the boy's mother.

The blond woman grabbed her son and started dragging him toward the door, but the boy shook himself loose.

"Don't worry, Viking." The Queen sneered. "The king has many whores. He can make more."

# BACK TO THE SHIPS

Olaf hated hearing people talk in a language he couldn't understand, so he rode Wid's little Highland Pony far in front of the cart, even though he often had to drop back and ask Wid for directions.

Wid the trader couldn't help himself. "Tell Jarl Olaf that the pony suits him. And if he's interested in her, I'll make him a good deal."

Tor ignored him.

"I told you I could get you to the king." Apparently, Wid was uncomfortable with silence. Not the type of man Tor would drink with.

Olaf wanted to go faster, but Wid warned him against it. "The bogs could swallow a horse and cart and everyone in it. Best to let the ponies feel if the ground is stable or sinking."

That Tor did translate for Olaf, who grudgingly let his pony slip to the rear.

Tor considered how to best deal with the sheriff and retrieve the stone. *Go in heavy handed, like a raid, or attempt diplomacy? Olaf is going to want to raid. So are the men.* But sacking the town and killing Picts wouldn't help them prove themselves particularly good allies. No, if they raided Scone, Drest's men would likely cut their throats before they made it to the Highlands.

"The King lent you his son," Wid rattled on. "I told you he trusted me."

*I wonder if the boy would agree with that.* Tor decided it

was time to test his hunch.

"Orri?" Tor leaned toward the nervous-looking prince. Then in Norse he asked, "Ever been on a longship, before?"

The boy shook his head, then looked down at his feet. "I-I don't understand," he stammered in the Pictish tongue.

Tor looked at the boy with a twisted smile. *That's all it took?* The boy was about as likely to keep a secret as Wid was to lose money.

"Ha!" Olaf's heels nearly dragged the ground as he brought the pony up next to the cart. "Where are you from then? Are you Norse or Dane?"

"Neither—"

Tor stared at the boy.

Olaf laughed and jerked young Orri onto his lap, kicking and screaming. "Ja Wid, your friend the king has lent us his spy." Olaf smacked the struggling boy in the back of his neck with his hand. "I don't know which one of the Pict's I should kill first. What do you think, Tor?"

In case the squirming Wid planned to jump, Tor wrapped his arm around the trader's neck and squeezed tight. Wid's bones cracked like a church door's hinges.

"Wait!" screamed Orri. "My mother is a slave!"

"What difference should that make to us?" Olaf leaned his elbow on Orri's back.

"Drest took her after a failed Viking raid. She's Norse, like you."

"So, you're a Northman then?" Tor guessed it was something like that.

"Half, I guess," Orri tried to explain. "The King is my father, but he has another family. A real one." Orri fell limp like a dead deer across Olaf's lap.

"Do you think that's supposed to buy you our sympathy?" Olaf smacked him on the rump. "A third of our crew are illegitimate, whether they realize it or not."

## HOW UBBI LOST HIS TONGUE

"I swear, Jarl Olaf," Orri pleaded, "if you promise to take my mother and me back to Norway, I will help you."

Tor rolled his eyes. "Take your mother—? Boy, we want to ally with your father against the Gaels, not start a war with the Picts over a slave." Wid had stopped struggling. Tor shook the man's head. The trader was breathing but unresponsive, so he shoved him into the back of the cart.

"The best thing we can do is lock you up until we exact your father's toll from the sheriff. Then, if there's bloodshed, you tell your father the sheriff started it, or we'll tell him you tried to get us to steal you and your mother back to Norway."

"This isn't the first time my father's tried to get that holy stone," said Orri. "The sheriff will fight you, and if you kill the villagers, then my father's hands will be clean. Do you really think he'll pick a fight with the Gaels for this? Once he has the stone, he'll probably kill you and claim he saved it from a failed Viking raid."

The boy liked to talk, that was clear.

"Holy stone?" Tor looked at Olaf. "This does feel suspicious. Why would Drest need us unless he's saving face or doesn't want to lose his own men?"

"I dunno, and I don't care. This is why I'm the Jarl, Tor. You're too easy to manipulate." Olaf picked the skinny boy up by his breeches and threw him back in the cart, driving the disoriented Wid back to the floor. Amidst the jerking knees and thrown elbows, Tor learned a few Pict curse words he hadn't heard before. "Try to escape and I'll snap your neck like a twig."

"The sheriff's son is my friend," Orri grunted. "If I can get you the stone, with no bloodshed, will you let me help my mother? We won't eat much. My father barely gives us enough to eat as it is."

"You're a Pict, boy. And you'll spend your life in Pictavia as a tool of your father." Olaf smiled a gap-toothed grin. "Besides, have you ever been to Norway?"

"No," Orri admitted.

"Whether by axe or cold, you wouldn't survive your first winter."

Ahead, the dragon-headed ships were silhouetted against a gray evening sky. The fires were burning, and the smell of roasting venison filled the air. Mead horns clanked amidst the laughter of men.

"Olaf," said Tor, "we've got some planning to do. The guards can watch the prince for the night."

# MEETING UBBI

Ubbi circled the skinny Pict. Right away, he didn't like the look of him.
"So, who are you?"
"Orri." The Pict pushed his long, greasy hair out of his face, as if proud that he couldn't grow a beard. Ubbi stroked the hairs he'd cultivated on his own chin. "What are you, stable boys?"
Ubbi punched Orri in the back of the head. "Mind your tongue, Pict. We din' ask to be your babysitter."
Orri rubbed his head and gave Ubbi a dirty look.
*That skinny little-* Ubbi raised his hand again.
"My father is Drest," blurted Orri, "King of the Picts."
"Yeah, right. We take care of all the royalty, don't we, Njáll?"
Ubbi kneed Orri in the thigh.
"Aagh!" Orri went down. Then the skinny scrapper grabbed Ubbi by the leg, driving him down into a thicket of bracken fronds. He only landed one blow before Ubbi flipped him over, pinned him on his back, and boxed him on the ears.
Njáll hawked up phlegm and got ready to let it sing.
"My mother's a slave." Orri cringed. "I'm as much Norse as I am Pict."
"Looks like a Pict to me." Ve, another boy, pushed Njáll and his dangling gob of snot aside.
"You've got to take me to Tor and Olaf," Orri begged. His eyes fixed on Njáll, the spitter.
"You don't understand, *Pict*. Nobody wants to see you.

Olaf don't want to see you. Tor don't want to see you. Even your father don't want to see you, or—"

"He wouldn't have left me with you." Orri finished Ve's sentence.

"Ubbi," Ve said. "Keep holding 'im down while Njáll coughs up another oyster."

"If they raid that village, they'll lose a lot of men."

"Did you mention your concern for our safety while you were riding in Tor's cart?" Ubbi asked.

"Of course," said Orri.

"Well, your highness," Njáll bowed, "you tried your best, and Tor could smell the shite on your breath as easy as the rest of us. So, while they drink the mead and plan the raid, you're stuck wif us—"

"Like one of the ponies." Orri finished his sentence, again.

Njáll hawked up another.

"Have you got a head cold or something?" Ubbi gagged. "If I throw up, I'm going to sink you neck deep in the moors and leave you for the banshees."

"They're the ones that scream and wail, right?" Ve looked like he was straining his brain.

Orri nodded vigorously, his eyes fixated on Njáll.

"See, I told you banshees were real." Ve stared at Orri's pale face. "Even the Pict's afraid."

"He's only afraid someone's going to spit into that big mouth of his. Anyway, Ve, why would I be afraid of wailing witches?" Njáll laughed. "I've known your mother since I was six years old."

Ubbi crushed Orri's shoulders into the ground before letting him back to his feet. "I am no stable boy." Ubbi pointed to the sword belted on his waist. *He* wouldn't be sleeping with horses much longer.

"Listen," Orri said, "there's a reason my father wants you to go into that village instead of sending his own men. A lot of people are going to die…Vikings and Picts alike."

## HOW UBBI LOST HIS TONGUE

"Do you think a man like Olaf is going to disgrace himself on the word of some chicken prince?" Ve asked. "In case you didn't know, we're here to borrow an army–"

"And that means we're not afraid to fight," Njáll finished his sentence.

"Are you two related?"

Ubbi wondered if all Picts had balls as big as this one, or if it was just his Norse side talking. "Your king would be smart to ally with us. If Olaf and Tor don't bring a Pict army north, they might end up bringing a Gael army south. I'm not sure we'd be able to tell the difference."

Orri shook his head. "You need not raid. Don't you see? I have a friend in the village, the sheriff's very own son. My father wants a stone, and I can get it for you."

"If you could get it, then he wouldn't be sending us, stupid." Njáll tried slapping Orri's head, but the Pict was as quick as he was skinny.

"Leave him alone." Ubbi shoved Njáll back. "There'll be nothing left of him come morning if we keep slapping him around all night."

"But it's all right when you do it, ja?" Njáll put his chest into Ubbi's. Njáll was a berserker in the making, but he hadn't grown into his balls yet.

"Are you going on the raid?" Orri asked.

"No." Ve seemed happy for the distraction. "They need us to guard the ponies."

"And the ships." Njáll grudgingly stepped away from Ubbi.

Ubbi waved away the stench of cod that lingered from Njáll's breath.

Ubbi put his hand on the hilt of his sword. "I'll probably go. Tor gave me this sword himself, before we left Norway."

"Yeah, right. You only got that sword because you'd already mastered the oar." Njáll was an idiot.

"Oh, I'm going!" Ubbi wasn't sure he was, but he

wanted Njáll to know he wasn't afraid.

"We are Vikings," Ve clarified to Orri, "but we're still training."

Ubbi wished Ve would stop explaining that to people. The only person that line fooled was Ve—and maybe his mother.

"Pict boys *and girls* get their training on the battlefield." Orri puffed out a chest that looked as hollow as a soup bowl.

"Hmph," Njáll chortled. "Trained to hide in the trees when there's trouble. And stab half-dead Vikings in the back." Njáll really hated Picts.

Ubbi remembered when the men in the village would tell stories of the blue-faced crazies slipping in and out of the trees, never holding still long enough for them to form a shield wall. When they were all younger, Njáll used to admit those stories gave him nightmares. Ubbi had always heard Njáll's mother might have been a Pict. He tried to picture him with a painted blue face.

"Vikings don't go into battle until they're strong enough to break Picts' necks with their bare hands." Little Ve needed to leave the tough talk to Njáll.

"I guess enough time rowing the boats will give you a strong grip." Orri looked to be bracing for impact.

Ubbi put his hand on Njáll's chest to stop him from throwing a punch. There were many reasons why this lot was still watching the ponies.

"Listen." Orri seemed determined to win the argument or get his teeth knocked out trying. "Even if they succeed, Tor and Olaf may never make it out of my father's hall if they take the stone by force. Some of my father's best men are from that clan... and every Pict believes in the power of that stone." Orri stared at Ubbi as if to give that time to sink in. He could wait all night for Njáll and he'd never get the point. "If Tor and Olaf won't listen, then it's up to us."

"Us?" Ubbi stepped away from the idiot. If the Pict

## HOW UBBI LOST HIS TONGUE

wanted Njáll to beat him so badly, he was done getting in the way.

"If you boys can find riders for each of those ponies, preferably at least one more with a sword, we can be back with the stone by morning—with no bloodshed."

Njáll looked up like he was counting in his head. Then, as if the math was too hard, he went back on the offensive. "A stone? I'm not sure you know how this works, Pict. We raid for silver."

"Njáll, do you need a nap?" Ubbi redirected Njáll's anger before he drowned Orri in a bog.

"Tor and Olaf were told it was just some ancient artifact," Orri explained, "but to Picts it's worth more than silver, or gold. Legend has it, it's a key to the Fae world. It's the one thing in that village that really matters."

"I guess we'll see what the Picts hold so dear tomorrow, when Tor and Olaf bring it back after the raid, then."

For some reason, Orri wanted to convince Ubbi, as if his vote could sway the others.

"None of you will be safe if they shed blood to get that stone," Orri warned. "If not from Picts, then from the Fae. Tor's concerned about it, too. I heard him trying to reason with Olaf. He's a smart one, that one is. But the giant seems to want to make a name for himself."

"And he will, too. Both of 'em will. Maybe this is the raid that'll make us all famous." Njáll lifted his chin as if he could hear his father saying he was proud of him for the first time.

"Let driving the Gaels out of the Southern Isles make them famous, not getting killed for stealing a rock for my father." Orri spoke to Ubbi as if all their fates hung on *his* decision. "It doesn't get dark for a couple of hours. We can fix this tonight. Just get me to the village and I'll walk into that church, say my prayers, and walk out with the stone. Then you can give it to Tor and Olaf, and when they hand it to my father, you will share in their glory. You'll have tales to tell, other than how hard it was collecting wood for the fires."

Njáll laughed. "Did you say something about faeries? Will there be leprechauns, too?"

"Leprechauns?" Orri looked at Njáll as if he was a little slow. "I mean... Maybe? It's said that Christ himself snatched the stone away from Brigid."

Now they were expected to know Pictish folklore.

"Brigid, the Pict Goddess...?" Orri gave them an incredulous stare. Ubbi just shrugged. He had no idea who she was. "It would be like Christ taking Thor's hammer," Orri added.

Ve swore under his breath and Njáll's mouth fell open.

"It was that show of power that caused my people to convert to Christianity. Just wait, he'll conquer your gods, too."

Njáll jerked the Pict around by the shoulder. "Maybe your slave mother hasn't taught you about our gods. In the North, we worship at the altar of war. Our gods have ravens, not doves. They respect revenge, not forgiveness. Thor's a giant killer. I don't think he will give up his hammer to your *Jesus* anytime soon."

"My father is the King," Orri snapped. "He never afforded me the luxury of faith in any god or anyone, except my mother. And that's why I intend to fix this tonight."

*What were they getting involved in?*

"Listen. It would be a miracle if Vikings handed that stone to my father, and that's what it needs to look like — like it was willed to my father by God, himself. Heck, if we pull this off, I might even start to believe."

"What's in this for you?" Ubbi asked.

"If I can fix this, I'm hoping Tor might convince Olaf to take me and my mother back to Norway...and maybe I'll earn the respect of my father."

"What do you expect? For us to steal a ship?" Njáll

## HOW UBBI LOST HIS TONGUE

asked.

"No." Orri seemed surprised at the question, but not as surprised as Ubbi.

"Wait, Njáll. We're not—"

"We only need the ponies—three, four hours at the most—but only if you're Vikings." Orri put on a solemn tone as effortlessly as he might a clean shirt. "We don't need stable boys."

"There's no way we're doing this." Ubbi couldn't believe they were listening to this weasel.

"Ubbi," Njáll said. "Aren't you always saying we must make a bold move if we want to get noticed? We don't have fathers on these ships. We haven't any advocates at Olaf's table."

"Are *you* siding with this Pict now?" Ubbi's eye twitched.

"Maybe we should," Ve said.

Orri had gotten to them.

"I should've let Njáll break your jaw." Ubbi threw his hands in the air and glared at the Pict. "At least then you'd have lost the use of that silver tongue."

"We can come back if things look suspicious." Njáll picked up his axe. "This isn't about the Pict. Being bold will get us gold—probably even an arm ring." He threw a blanket over the back of a pony.

"Is it any different from what Tor and Olaf are doing?" Orri tried to reassure Ubbi. "Sailing down to Pictavia to negotiate with a foreign king? Do you think Tor and Olaf gave you that sword because you did what you were told? Do you think these boys will get swords by grooming the ponies and pulling oars?" Ubbi didn't answer, for that's exactly how he'd earned his iron. He really hated that Pict.

# SCONE

Ubbi cursed under his breath with every hoofbeat of his surefooted little pony.

Thanks to Njáll, their numbers had grown. He'd convinced Bjorn to come, who was the only one who'd been on a raid before, and Bjorn dragged one of his less sober friends, Haldor, to join the adventure too.

Bjorn nearly knocked Njáll off his pony when he figured out he'd left a cask of ale for what amounted to little more than a scouting mission. To bolster their spirits, Orri reminded the young Vikings of some of the things that could go wrong. Risk was an important ingredient for making any last minute, late night enterprise worth missing sleep over.

None of them had ever talked to a Pict before, or met one that spoke Norse. They took full advantage. At first, they passed the time airing grievances about the Pictish countryside. The complaints followed the passing of a skin of mead.

Haldor hated the constant rain, Ve the stench of the bogs, and Njáll joked about how convenient it was the way the wind got colder as the sun went down. None of that was any worse than back in Norway, but they weren't in Norway. So pretty much everything that wasn't gold or silver or looked good in a skirt was bound to reek as bad as Swedish Surströmming.

"And why do the men down 'ere wear dresses?" Njáll nearly choked on his ale.

Haldor laughed. "Ja, Pict or Gael, they all like their

## HOW UBBI LOST HIS TONGUE

skirts, don't they?"

"Maybe it's your mighty father's decree, eh, Pict?" Njáll prodded.

"And what's with the blue make-up?"

"Ja, ja. If it weren't for the beards, I'm not sure I could tell man from woman."

"They're called léines, not dresses," Orri snapped, for the first time rising to take the bait. "And if you wade through a few of these bogs, you'll wish you were wearing one, too."

"Enough!" Ubbi shoved Njáll, and he tumbled off his pony. He landed on his back with a squish and an exhaust of air. *Was he drunk?* "Leave the Pict alone before he steers us off course. I don't want to be navigating these moors without him. And lay off the drink."

Orri nodded at Ubbi as if he thought he'd made a friend. *Did he just wink?* Orri held up his chin a little higher and urged his pony on. "Won't be long now, lads. If we can get that stone tonight, maybe we'll get our own ship."

"Our own ship?" Bjorn grunted to help the breathless Njáll back on his horse. "You don't even have a sword."

"You think this will get us one?" Ve got excited. "If we get that stone, Tor's got to let us raid, won't he?"

"Tor? No. He's all about being strong, trained, and ready," Haldor said.

"Maybe a reward, then?" Njáll was the one dreaming, now.

"We're sneaking away to steal Olaf's glory and you're hoping for a prize?" Ubbi said. "I'm just hoping he doesn't give us his boot."

"Ought to earn us something, though, shouldn't it?" Ve's question hung in the air unanswered, like the fog on the moors.

*Good.* Ubbi was glad to have spoiled their speculating.

They'd been traveling for just over an hour under the light of a crescent moon. The light was cool but the night had turned muggy. Orri'd led them deep into the endless cesspools and stench, along trails unseen, breaks in the marshland grasses, and bracken that only he and the ponies could decipher from the rest. Ubbi wiped sweat from his brow. How ugly this place was compared to home. The whole of their trip could've been navigated in half the time after a good winter's freeze. A foot of snow, some skis, maybe a sled and some dogs.

Ubbi missed home. They'd been gone too long.

Instead, they traveled the mire, having to listen to this Pict tell them when to ride and when to walk—or prattle on about the depths of the moors or the dangers of getting lost in the fog.

"Close enough." Orri dismounted. "Stay here and stay quiet. The village is just on the other side of those trees. I won't be long."

The Northmen looked at each other, as confused as if the Pict had just taken out his left eye.

"Oh no, no, no. Do you think we're going to sit here while you go into one of your Pict villages—alone?" Njáll jumped off his pony and stepped between Orri and the village.

"He'd turn us in. We'd be hanging from a tree by morning."

Ve and the others dismounted, encircling the Pict like he'd planned to set them up the whole time. *Maybe he had.* Ubbi watched as his friends turned their scowls at each other, like they were looking for the one who'd agreed to this stupid idea in the first place.

Only then did Ubbi realize the position they'd put themselves in. He broke the silence before they threw punches. "We can still go back. No one has to know."

"You're acting like scared pups," Orri chided.

Ubbi wished he'd been paying more attention when Orri described all the ways Picts had died in the moors.

"Now's not the time to be changing the plan."

# HOW UBBI LOST HIS TONGUE

"You had a plan," Ubbi reminded Orri. "*They* had drunk ambition."

"Well, we're sober now." Bjorn avoided looking at Njáll, who was still as lit as a yule log. "And I'm *not* going back without that stone."

*Stubborn oaf.*

"Me neither." Haldor crossed his arms.

"Well, I'm not sitting in the woods while the Pict gathers the villagers to hunt us like rabbits." Njáll glowered at Orri.

"If anybody's a rabbit, it's you." Bjorn punched him in the shoulder.

"Nobody's calling anyone a rabbit." Ubbi stared Bjorn down until he, and everybody else, shut up. "If we stay, we all go to the church, together."

Ve looked nervous. "But—"

Ubbi cut him off before he said something he'd never live down. "Ve, I need you to stay and watch the ponies. I promise you'll get equal credit."

"Well, I promise if you stay behind, you'll be known as Stable Boy for the rest of your life." Njáll burped, straightened his shirt, and wiped the sweat from his brow.

"I'm going." Ve's face looked like he'd eaten rotten fish.

Ubbi shook his head. Ve was only thirteen years old. Too young for any of this.

"Worst that can happen is we kill some Picts, right?" Ve's voice quavered like a child, assuring his friends he was no longer afraid of the dark.

"No." Njáll put his arm around Ve. "Worst that can happen is we share a beer in Odin's Hall tonight, while a Pictish witch stews our bones for supper."

"No riskier than going out to sea," said Bjorn. "We're all destined to die. Today or tomorrow—makes no difference to me."

"My lands. You Vikings are a dreary bunch, aren't you? Nobody need die tonight. If you had just let me go, I'd 'ave already been back with the stone by now. So, new plan—we *all* sneak in, *quietly*." Orri looked at Njáll as if wondering if he understood the concept. "Quietly, without weapons—"

"With weapons." Bjorn withdrew his sword. The others held up their seaxes and axes.

It was Orri's turn to shake his head in disbelief.

"We slip into the church, grab the stone, and come back here. We'll be back at the ships with five hours left to daylight."

Blank stares were all he got in return.

Ubbi knew these boys, and even a trip to the woods to drop trou didn't go *that* smoothly.

# CHURCHES, SKIRTS, AND EMPTY STREETS

The village was small and mostly quiet. As they passed through the open square, Ubbi got his bearings. There was a well, and next to that was the smith's forge. It wasn't too different than the square in his village back home. Smoke crept down the side of the chimney of a large wooden hall, filling the square like a low fog. The hairs stood up on his arms when he heard the murmur of Picts inside. *Should've waited a few hours before coming in. Stupid.*

"Aye!" Ve lunged back, knocking Bjorn into Ubbi, pinning his drawn sword to his chest.

Bjorn responded by shoving Ve into Njáll, knocking them both to the ground. The head of Ve's axe bounced against some iron bars laying at the foot of the smith's forge. The clanking iron cut into the quiet like a call to arms.

"I didn't mean to!" Ve pointed to rabbits and swamp rat carcasses, hooked and hanging out in the open air to age.

"Didn't you grow up on a farm?" Njáll climbed back to his feet.

Ubbi threw his hand over Njáll's mouth and pointed his sword toward the hall. The door creaked open, casting a narrow light to the opposite side of the square. The night filled with Pictish chatter, and two men stepped outside. Bjorn and Haldor slipped behind the forge, leaving the rest caught in the courtyard, still as stone. The Picts stared right past them.

Ubbi's hand shook from the weight of his sword, but he dared not let it fall. He dared not even breathe.

The Picts dropped trou and proceeded to water the grass.

After the door closed behind them, Ubbi inhaled for the first time since the axe fell.

Quiet as thieves, the squad followed Orri as he slipped between shadows toward the little church.

In and out, home in time for breakfast. The unlocked door creaked as they slipped inside, one by one.

"Cò tha ann?" a tired voice came from the other room.

Something else they hadn't considered. They didn't know the language. Ubbi wanted to smack Orri, but before he could, Bjorn and Njáll rushed a yawning priest and pinned him against the wall.

Bjorn stuck his sword to the priest's throat and started barking his demands... in Norse. "Where's the stone?"

The priest's disheveled hair thinly covered his wide eyes. With a whimper, he wet the nightshirt that failed to conceal the quaking of his knees.

"The stone, you idiot," Njáll's failed whisper rang off the rough stone walls. It reminded Ubbi of the way his father used to yell at the dogs to get them to stop barking at noises in the dark.

"Idiot." Ubbi grabbed Njáll by the collar and pushed him to the floor. "He's a Pict...he doesn't understand. Orri! Tell the pissing priest to keep quiet or Bjorn's going to cut his throat."

Bjorn's face turned white as the priest's shirt. He didn't seem ready to wet his blade on the helpless old fool.

They'd heard the battle worn, soulless old salts tell of running priests through like it was some sort of game. Didn't seem so glorious now that they could see the fear in his eyes. Is he praying? Ugh, that might make it easier.

Ubbi ran his fingers through the leather thong holding

his soul ring around his neck. That heavy mystery his own priest had cut so painfully from his adolescent chest. This whole expedition had it weighing on him like an anchor.

Bjorn had never used that sword to take a life before. Tor'd given it to him two raids past, but he'd never used it for anything other than making sure the battle corpses were actually...well, dead.

Tor always said, "The Valkyries won't take your soul if you're killed stealing from a coward pretending that he's dead."

Ubbi watched the others upending the church. Did they even know what they were looking for? A stone. The stone of Scone. The road was covered with them. Ubbi even had a few stuck in his boot.

"Orri, ask the priest where he hid the stone before Bjorn stains the floor with him." Ubbi tried to keep his voice low.

"Where's he at?" Ve asked.

Ubbi spun around to search the room. The large cross was leaning low against a table, some drawers had been rifled through, and Orri the Pict was gone.

"I'm going to kill that skinny, little maggot," Njáll announced a foolish, hollow threat.

"What are we going to do?" Ve sounded so small.

"We need to go back to the ships." Haldor looked nervous for the first time. Maybe he wasn't as ready to meet a Valkyrie as he'd been letting on.

"He's probably already knocking on the sheriff's door."

"Get the priest to tell us where the sheriff lives," said Njáll.

Ubbi grabbed Njáll by the shirt. "Did you get kicked in the head or something? He can't understand us, and we can't understand him." Ubbi couldn't figure out who the weakest link was, Njáll for not understanding that Picts couldn't speak Norse, or him for going along with this plan in the first place. The bastard Prince was right. They weren't Vikings—just a bunch of gullible stable boys.

Ubbi slammed the hilt of his new sword into the downed wooden cross. "If he wanted us caught, the men in the hall would've been here already. It's just a few doors down." Ubbi mopped the sweat from his brow. "You all stay here with the priest, try to get him to understand. All we want is the stone. Bjorn, if he tries to call for help then you're going to have to wet that blade. The rest of you just search. It's a magic stone, it'll probably be obvious when you see it."

"What are you going to do, Ubbi?"

Did Ve just wipe his eyes with his sleeve?

"I'm going to find Orri." Ubbi went into the back room and found the priest's clothes hanging on a chair. He shook his head as he swapped his shirt and trousers for the priest's skirt and robe. All he could do was shake his head. This was the kind of thing that gave a man a nickname for the rest of his life.

What would they say? Ubbi the priest? Ubbi short skirt? He had no choice. It was a little loose, but it would do. He stared at the door as if it led out onto thin ice. He cracked his knuckles and lumbered through. Before he left, he found the smallest Viking, Ve, and shoved his clothes in his hands. "Lose my clothes, and you're dead."

"Sorry ma'am, have you seen our friend, Ubbi?" Haldor's mocking couldn't hide the quake in his voice.

"Do you want to go out there?" Ubbi put his hand on the hilt of his sword, the way Tor always did. "I didn't think so. Seeing the priest walking around the village probably won't raise too much suspicion."

"Careful, miss." Bjorn chortled.

Ubbi didn't have time for these idiots. "If you know what's good for you, you'll never mention this to anyone — ever." He calmed, took a deep breath, and let all the tension out. "The stone is here, somewhere. Quietly — check everywhere. The priest may have it hidden between his cheeks for all we know."

## HOW UBBI LOST HIS TONGUE

Ve's jaw fell open, and he took a quick step away from the priest and the horrified Bjorn.

Now they knew how Ubbi felt about what he had to do next. Ubbi exhaled slowly, looked both ways, and stepped into the moonlight. Shadows stretched like napping ghosts along quiet, narrow streets.

Ubbi had no idea how to find Orri, but he guessed they hadn't passed the sheriff's house on the way into town or he might've mentioned it. Ubbi would have to go farther. Farther from the ships, farther from the ponies, and farther from his friends.

# THE SHERIFF'S SON

Ubbi pulled the priestly hood over his head and eased his way up the muddy road. His only peace was that he was walking away from the hall.

He didn't know what he expected to find, but he slowed outside of every door. The village started compact, but the land between the houses stretched more and more the higher up the hill he walked. A small winding creek gurgled beside the road to his left, and a short stone wall bordered his right. Cows gave him away with uneasy grunts and snorts as he passed.

He thought he might stop when he got to the house at the top of the hill and work his way back to the village. *What was he going to do, though? Knock on doors?* If he didn't spot Orri by the time he got back to the church, they'd have no choice but to leave, with or without the stone. *This is awful.* Then he realized it was worse than that. They may have lost the Pict King's son. He plopped down on the short border wall, put his head in his hands and leaned sideways against the pillar supporting the gate.

*Tor and Olaf are going to kill me.*

Something landed behind him. He looked up to see if it might be raining, but only a crescent moon and a field of stars stared back at him. The night sky was clear of clouds, leaving the surrounding area bright. Then a rock skipped down the road and hit him on the foot. His heart stopped. He was a sitting target. All he could think was to hide. *Like a little child.* He fell backward, landing on soft grass. The fall sent a swarm of flies from their warm perch, a pile of dung not a foot away from Ubbi's head. A cow spooked and ran away four paces before stopping to stare.

Then he heard the voices.

From his stomach, he pushed up to peek. Two figures were coming down the road, unaware. *Lucky.* Another stone skipped along the wall before hitting the cow and spooking the rest of the herd. Ubbi looked over his shoulder at the farmhouse in the distance and hoped they didn't have hounds.

The voices were getting closer.

*Too exposed.*

He tried to find a way to escape. The wall went straight back into the darkness. How far he couldn't tell, but too close to the farmhouse, either way. Pasture to one side and pasture to the other. If he ran, he'd be seen. If he stayed, all they'd have to do is look over their left shoulder when they passed, and he'd be caught.

He'd heard Picts were nasty folk. That if they caught a Northman anywhere near their village, they'd have his head on a pike.

Ubbi turned onto his side and slid his belly to the wall. The footsteps were so close he could feel them. He noticed the fog of his own breath. His heartbeat thumped inside his chest like a drum.

The stones were cool against his forehead. The air smelled like dung, and he wondered if the squish he'd felt under his hip was from a horse or a cow. In his mind, he begged them to hurry past. For all he knew they'd seen him earlier, and they were discussing how stupid the Northman must be to think he could hide behind so short a wall.

If I could just understand what they were saying.

"If you can help us get the stone, we can stop this feud," one voice said in the cryptic Pictish tongue. "My father always respected your father, but he can't accept open defiance. He wants that stone."

"And he's willing to sacrifice us all to get it?"

"I don't think he's sacrificing me." There was a long pause. "All right. I guess so, yes."

After the voices finally passed, Ubbi sucked in the cool night air like a drink of fresh water. He couldn't believe his luck. It was Orri. Ubbi got up out of the muck. Disgusted and angry, he rolled—belly down—over the short wall, and, as quietly as he could, eased his sword out of its sheath.

He thought about that sword. He could've never afforded to buy it on his own. It was a signal, from Tor, that he was ready. Tomorrow might've been his first raid. He could've arrived in Scone with Tor and Olaf, and he'd betrayed that trust.

Because of that Pict, he was alone, covered in dung, and hiding like a child playing games with his friends. How fitting that the first blood his new sword might draw would be Orri's.

Ubbi eased up behind the boys, grabbed one by the hair and stuck the tip of his sword into the dimple between the top of his neck and the base of his skull.

"One of you better start speaking Norse."

"Whoa, whoa, whoa." Orri jumped forward, leaving his friend behind.

He must've run ten strides before stopping.

"Ubbi?" Orri squinted to see better, then lowered his hands and raised a smile. "This is one of the Viking stable boys," Orri explained—in Pict.

Ubbi pulled back on the other's hair until he dropped to his knees. "If I hear that language spoken one more time, I'm going to push this blade until it comes out one of your friend's eyes."

"What would you have me do? You don't speak Pict, and he doesn't speak Norse." Orri was entirely too comfortable considering his friend was about to die.

## HOW UBBI LOST HIS TONGUE

Ubbi knew he should probably just kill them both, collect the others, and head back to the ships. *No. Too late for that.* The priest had seen. By morning, the village would be on alert for an attack.

"This is Oengus, the sheriff's son." He introduced the boy to Ubbi as if they were meeting over a beer. "I-I wasn't leaving you," Orri explained. "When I didn't see the stone in the church, I knew Oengus would know where it was. He's on my side, Ubbi."

"But who's side are you on?"

"Yours," Orri said before the stupid smile fell off his face. "Well, mine. Look, I told you, my mother's a slave, and that stone can buy her escape. If I can save my friend's stubborn father from getting his entire village killed in a Viking raid while doing it, then all the better."

The sheriff's son started rattling off Pictish.

Ubbi panicked, jerked back on his hair, and moved his blade around to the front of his throat. "Tell your friend to shut his mouth."

"This disagreement is between a sheriff and his king, not us," Orri said. "Oengus will help us."

"I don't trust him." Ubbi didn't trust his friends either. Who knew what they were doing in his absence? "You can tell me everything on our way back to town. And I promise if either of you tries anything, I'll cut your legs out from under you." Ubbi stared at Orri. "Well, go ahead. Translate. But be quick about it. Your words hurt my ears, like a couple of cackling hens."

Orri said enough to get them walking, then Ubbi cut them off. "What's so special about the stone...? Is it some kind of gem?"

"No. Nothing like that." Orri turned and started walking backwards. "Ever hear of David and Goliath?" Ubbi let Orri explain everything as they made their way back into town. It was hard to concentrate knowing he could be walking into a trap, but he tried to remember some of what was said. Ubbi figured it might be valuable to report something he'd learned to Tor and Olaf if he ever made it back.

It turned out, Scone wasn't worth raiding. But Ubbi didn't need anyone to tell him that. If it was iron and silver they were after, Perth, a city just across the river, was a much better target. Scone was just some holy place to the ancient Picts. Somewhere they could meet their old gods. But their Pope didn't like that, so he built a worthless little church and put one of his holy relics in it to turn it into a Christian holy site. The stone they were after was one of five picked up by a boy to kill a giant.

It was the giant-killing stone King Drest wanted.

Ubbi felt the weight of his new sword in his hand. One Viking corralling two Picts down a road, uncontested. *Stupid Christians. It takes iron to kill giants.* He thought of Olaf. What would the Picts do when Olaf came to raid? *I doubt they'd go around picking up stones to stop him.*

"If I see you taking us anywhere near that hall, I'll—"

"I know, you'll cut off our legs," Orri said and turned to translate it. Oengus grunted before leading them through back alleys to get to the back of the church.

The door creaked open. *Empty. Could my luck be any worse?* "Where are they?"

"Maybe they got the priest to give them the stone," Orri suggested in a cool voice. "They might be halfway to the ships by now."

Ubbi's pulse pounded in his temples. "Alright, but the sheriff's son is coming with us."

Orri cast a glance at his friend.

"Don't worry. If we get that stone, you have my word he will be safe." Ubbi looked around the church as Oengus tried to right the tilted wooden cross. What a disappointment. His first raid and he was leaving empty-handed. Not even a stupid rock.

# THE STONE OF DAVID

The sheriff's son led Ubbi and Orri out the back door of the church. They darted from house to house, like a rock across the pond, only touching down to take cover behind a fence or building.

The jeers of a crowd echoed eerily through the streets. The hair stood up on Ubbi's arms.

"There's something happening outside the hall," said Orri.

"I have ears." Ubbi didn't need a translator to figure out something, or someone, had roused the village's ire.

The sheriff's son turned to Orri and said something Pictish, and before Ubbi could stop him, he was running toward the jeers.

Had the sheriff noticed his son was missing? Had Tor and Olaf come? Ubbi figured he was dead either way. All he could do was make the most out of what he still had. He stuck the tip of the sword in Orri's back. "If the sheriff's son betrays us, I'm going to run you through, Pict."

"He won't." Orri's voice quaked, which was reassuring. "If he does, I'm in as much trouble as you are. He wants us to go back to the church."

Ubbi cracked his neck.

"Listen, before you jumped out of the mire, Oengus told me the stone is framed in gold. It may be hanging on the wall or something. Let's give it one last look to keep us busy while we wait." Orri gave a pleading look. "Trust me."

As if not getting stabbed was a sign of Ubbi's consent, Orri tiptoed off through the shadows and disappeared back into the church.

Again, Ubbi was alone. *I'm going to kill these Picts.* The echoes grew louder. Angrier. Maybe Tor and Olaf had come. All the more reason he needed to stick close to Orri. The Pict King may have wanted the stone, but, just as important, they needed to bring back his son. By the time he got inside, he found Orri kneeling in the front of the church. He wasn't praying, but holding a candle up close to an etching on the pulpit.

Orri swung his candle back and forth, inspecting every detail. A glimmer behind the pulpit caught Ubbi's eye. Then with a shift of the candle, it disappeared.

There was a painting along the walls of the little church, in panels, like pictures made to tell a story. Scanning the room, Ubbi saw that it started above the main entrance. The first panel was of a man and woman, clothed in leaves, holding a fruit, and talking to a serpent. After was an ugly, large ship with no oars and no sail, bobbing alone in rough seas. On the opposite wall, near the back door where the cross had stood before the search for the stone, there was a picture of the Christ dying on a cross. After that, there was one of women talking to a winged figure painted in brilliant white, sitting atop a stone next to what looked to be a cave. The panels kept wrapping around until the last showed a battle of angels and demons. All Vikings knew the story of the Christian Revelation, which was kind of like Ragnarök. *One of the few Christian stories worth repeating.*

He'd heard many of the stories in the panels told by captured monks and Christian slaves...sometimes they were the last stories they ever told.

Ubbi focused on the story behind the pulpit where Orri was frantically running his fingers back and forth along a gold leafed cross, as if trying to will the stone into

## HOW UBBI LOST HIS TONGUE

existence. The panel depicted a boy with a sling and stone standing over the body of a giant.

With a shift of Orri's candle, Ubbi saw the glint of gold again.

*No, couldn't be.*

But if it was, he wanted to be the one to give it to Olaf. He had a reputation to build, after all. Orri was already the son of a King. People like him didn't have to earn their respect. Or their swords.

"Any luck?" Ubbi needed Orri gone.

"No." Orri rubbed his eyes. "I don't understand. Oengus said it'd be at the pulpit."

"The blue paint you Pict's like to wear has made you blind." Ubbi jerked Orri to his feet. "Let me have a look."

Orri stretched his back.

"Well, I'll not have you standing there ready to stab me in the neck. Look outside to see where the sheriff's son took off to." Then he mumbled, "If he's bringing back a mob, maybe you can flap that tongue of yours and buy us some time to escape."

"He hasn't betrayed me," Orri said, though he seemed to be trying to reassure himself instead of Ubbi. "Oengus would rather buy his family favor with my father than see them skewered by you Vikings in a raid."

Ubbi didn't answer and Orri finally shut his big mouth and disappeared out the back door.

Ubbi went right to work. He dragged the priest's high-backed chair under the picture of the giant—embedded in a little yellow frame, like a gold halo marking where it had struck the giant on the forehead.

*There it is.*

The light was dim, but even he could see there was nothing special about it, just a smooth stone the size of the end of his thumb. The kind you could find in any creek from Pictavia to Norway.

Ubbi pulled out his seax and cut the whole thing right

out of the fabric. Working on top of the pulpit, with a little jiggering, Ubbi relieved the stone from its gold frame. He looked around for a safe place to hide it.

Shaking off his boot, Ubbi poured five stones into the palm of his hand, each only half as irritating as Orri. He compared them to the *special* stone and couldn't tell the difference. Quickly he put his stones onto the pulpit, held the gold frame over the one that looked like it might best fit, and cracked it in place with the end of the hilt.

He felt the weight of the stone that supposedly brought down a giant in the palm of his hand.

Hearing the door, Ubbi plopped it down into the wineskin hanging around his waist.

"What are you doing?" Orri asked.

"I found it."

"Give it to me," said Orri.

Ubbi felt his jaw tighten. *I wonder if my seax could cut out his attitude as easily as it had that stone?* "You can have the stone, but I'm keeping the gold." He couldn't risk handing him a stone that didn't fit exactly in the frame, so he pinned the tip of his seax in the gap and whacked it on the hilt with his palm.

Ubbi bit the gold, smiled, put it in his pocket, and left the stone on the pulpit for Orri.

"You really are just a stable boy, aren't you?" Orri looked disappointed. "Are you sure this is it?"

"You tell me, Pict."

"I wish you would stop calling me that. I am half Norse…my mother was the daughter of a Jarl."

"Your father's a Pict, isn't he?"

"My father's a king."

"Pffft." Ubbi wanted to distract Orri from questioning the stone. Truth was, he was jealous. He barely knew his own father. "I found the stone up there, wrapped in gold and sown into that mural—just like your friend said." Ubbi glanced out the back door. The air was thick with smoke and the ruckus of jeering men. "We've got what we came for. Let's try to find the others."

# PYRE IN THE SQUARE

Orri led Ubbi through the shadows, but all roads seemed to lead them back toward the sounds of drunken, jeering Picts.

As they eased closer, the orange glow of fire emanated from the square, casting ghostly shadows against the surrounding buildings. Ubbi's pulse quickened along with the rising clamor. He felt like he was spying on a coven of witches crying out for some meat to add to the pot. Witches might be preferable to what he thought might actually be happening.

He could see an outline of trees in the distance, and all of his senses were pulling him in that direction. The dangers of navigating the moors and bogs of Pictavia at night were preferable to finding out what had gotten the Picts so riled up. He thought he knew.

They passed an alley and glimpsed a nightmare. Ubbi pulled on his collar to let the night air cool his burning skin. There in the center of town, in front of what looked like a funeral pyre, Bjorn, Haldor, Ve, and Njáll were on their knees, gagged and bound. Their hands were tied in front of their stomachs, but they were bound together by what looked to be a heavy tree limb that had been driven between their backs and their elbows.

Two Picts on either side steered the pole, and his friends' faces, back and forth to give each of them a chance to taste the fire. The smaller two, Ve and Njáll, were in the middle and seemed to have it the worst. They never entirely left the heat or the smoke as the Picts pushed the

## HOW UBBI LOST HIS TONGUE

pole back and forth like they were cooking pigs on a skewer. Bjorn and Haldor were on the outside, most of the red on their faces was from trying to pull the others away from the fire.

"The sheriff's son..." whispered Ubbi. "He's betraying us now."

"That's his father." Orri put his hand on Ubbi's sword arm as if the weasel could hold him back. "They're arguing."

Though he cast an enormous shadow, the sheriff wasn't a large man. His head was bald, shoulders pointy, and he had a paunch like a pregnant woman. But his voice was cruel and loud.

Ubbi thought about ramming his sword down the weakling's throat. "What's he saying?"

The sheriff's son shoved the men steering the pole back from the fire. A moment of relief for his half-roasted friends.

"Oengus is defending them—explaining to his father that they're only here for the stone, that King Drest had sent them to bring it back without bloodshed."

Ubbi grabbed Orri by the collar, his face burning like the orange of the flames.

"You're the one who said we could get it without bloodshed. Ask young Ve how that's working out."

Orri knocked his hand away. Surprisingly strong for such a wiry runt.

The sheriff berated Oengus, chasing him around the fire like he was trying to lose a boot up his backside.

Ubbi didn't need to know the language to recognize a father embarrassing his son in front of God and prisoner alike.

Orri winced. But the women and children and old men around the fire started laughing.

"What?"

"The sheriff said he wished Oengus had been born a

girl. At least then he could marry him off and die knowing there was a set of balls there to watch after his grandchildren."

"At least he didn't send him off to die with some Vikings like yours did, eh?"

If Orri's eyes were knives, they'd have cut Ubbi's throat. Then his stare softened. "Your friends killed the priest."

"Fenrir, Jörmungandr, and Hella!" Ubbi put his head in his hand. *Idiots!* He didn't question whether it was true.

"He says your friends were scouting the village before a raid." Orri didn't take his eyes off Oengus, who was crawling back toward his house at the coaxing of his father's boot. "The sheriff's already sent a war party up the river." His eyes opened wide. "They're on their way to the ships."

Ubbi didn't know what to do. They'd never get back in time to warn Tor and Olaf. His stomach roiled as the flames licked at Ve's legs. The boy's face boiled with sweat and anguish. A gag stifled his screams. Ubbi choked the hilt of his sword. "I only see six of them. Most of the able men are probably heading upriver. If I can just get Bjorn free—"

The sheriff swung his sword down and took Bjorn's right arm off at the elbow. Bjorn let out a muffled roar and dropped to his face. The stroke took the man holding that end of the pole by surprise, sending him to the ground, too.

*No.* This was not the way this was supposed to go. This was a nightmare every Norse boy bragged would never happen to them. To die in battle meant Valhalla, but to die like a dog, without a weapon in your hand, meant Hel.

Even through the gag, Bjorn's screams were terrible, but he proved he was no dog when he put his hand down and clambered to his feet. The pole bearer remained down in the dirt, complaining in his Pictish tongue to the sheriff.

## HOW UBBI LOST HIS TONGUE

He was ignored.

"We've got what we came for." Orri held up the counterfeit stone. "If the war party follows the river, we may be able to beat them back to the ships to warn your Viking friends."

Ubbi couldn't believe this Pict. "Tor and Olaf can take care of themselves." He stood up straight, cracked his neck, and kissed his soul ring.

*Hail Thor!* It was as close to a prayer as he could muster as he pushed Orri aside and ran in to the square. He never really liked Bjorn, but he wouldn't sneak away with this Pict while they butchered his crew like cattle.

He had never killed before, but now the bloodlust boiled inside him. Tor had deemed him worthy to fight when he gave him a sword, and by the gods he would wet it with Pict blood this night.

But Bjorn wasn't finished yet. His hands were still tied together, and with a berserker's heart he grabbed the wrist of his dismembered arm and knocked the complaining Pict into the fire with his own bloody elbow. It might as well have been Thor's hammer. Bjorn wouldn't die unarmed today.

Ubbi stained his iron for the first time by disemboweling a useless elder that was watching the torture from outside the hall. The man spilled his guts before spilling his beer, without even realizing there was going to be a fight. The sword that Ubbi'd sharpened every day cut easily through rib and bowel, dropping the old goat like a fish tossed to shore. As soon as he'd made it to the square, he saw there were more than the six men he'd seen from the alley, and he'd need more help than he could expect from Bjorn One Arm, who was...already down.

Haldor, Njáll, and even Ve were doing everything they could to get in the fight. They'd made it to their feet, and Haldor was using rowing commands to synchronize their attack. Still bound to the pole, they managed to use it to knock a few Picts down, until a man wearing too short a skirt jumped on the pole where Bjorn used to be. Ve and Njáll stumbled under the weight, and as their side of the pole went down, the man's skirt flipped up, exposing his pale, red-haired cheeks to complement the waning moon.

Two old men grabbed Haldor's end of the pole, but somehow he kept his feet, dragging them back and forth in a semi-circle until a fat woman jumped on his back, driving the entire row of Vikings face first into the hard packed earth.

*No chance of unraveling that mess.* Ubbi changed his focus to the sheriff.

In a melee, Tor had trained them to take the fight to the closest armed man. But it was the leader's job to seek out the leader of the opposing force. Ubbi would cut the head off the snake, in hopes the rest of the villagers would retreat into their homes in the chaos.

Never rest your sword. Kill everything on your way.

Years of training took over. Someone slashed a rake at him. Ubbi slipped past, raised his sword, and drove it halfway into another's neck. A woman with three blue fingers of paint smeared down her cheeks charged him, her sharp nails scratching at his face.

She tried to cut off Ubbi's toes with a hoe, but when he finally jerked the sword free, it slashed the side of her knee. She dropped as fast as the man with a cleaved throat. A boy trying to act brave went down by a wound to the ankle, and a lucky drunk swinging a wooden cup stumbled back just before having the hand holding his beer cut off at the wrist.

Ubbi felt like a true warrior. Using a blade was even easier than Tor's sword training with wooden sticks. Already, Ubbi'd learned that a cut across the leg dismantled an enemy as fast as a kill, and often barely slowed his sword if he slashed shallow enough to avoid the bone. He could've been raiding all this time. He thought of all the wealth he'd missed out on. And how his first village had to be this one. Broke, except for the gold trim of a religious artifact.

The sheriff was waiting, sword still covered in Bjorn's blood. The lazy bugger didn't even run in to meet Ubbi's challenge. Ubbi was dog-tired, but already looking forward to telling Tor and Olaf the story of how he claimed Bjorn's revenge in the battle of Scone.

The paunch bellied sheriff stepped out of the way of Ubbi's downward stroke and the shock of no contact sent Ubbi tripping until he splayed out on the dirt. The worthless Pict had had the benefit of seeing his enemy's approach. Ubbi slammed his fists down hard into the dirt. First, he would take off that sword hand, then the other. Maybe leave the sheriff alive so his son would have to feed and clean him for the rest of his miserable life.

Ubbi seethed as he pushed up, but got tackled by an old man, then another. The boy he'd maimed ended up on his sword arm, biting down on his hand like a wild dog until he finally let it go. Ubbi struggled to get back to his sword, but there were too many of them. Fists and rocks rained down harder than a hailstorm.

One of the Picts smacked him on top of the head with Bjorn's severed arm. The flailing wrist cracked, then the world faded to black.

When he awoke, his head throbbed, and his mouth was dry. His wrists burned like fire. They'd tied him to Bjorn's spot on the pole, still sticky with his blood. Ubbi would've done anything to understand what the sheriff was saying, and he would've given twice as much to have not been there to see what came next.

# LOST BOYS

Ubbi slipped in and out of consciousness. A couple of old witches with blue stripes painted across their mouths each took their turn grabbing him by the hair and then slowly, almost sacrificially, cutting him down the face. They hovered the blade in front of his eyes to make sure he saw it coming before they raked it down his cheeks. Ubbi's teeth cracked in his head as he ground them together to keep from crying out in front of his friends. Tears washed his wounds, and the taste of blood fouled his lips. The feeling of each cut reminded him of the day his Gothi removed his soul. Just like then, he didn't want anyone to see the pain.

The sheriff said something, then motioned for a wiry onlooker. The man planted his cheek beside Ubbi's, forcing him to watch, as one by one, the sheriff murdered Ubbi's friends. The man's thin, scratchy beard irritated Ubbi's sliced cheeks. He smelled sweet, like honey mead.

The sheriff stabbed Haldor in the belly, and then the other Picts took their turns. When they cut him from the pole he was lost and started crawling toward the hall. No one tried to stop him. He was teetering by the time they turned their focus to Njáll.

When they cut Njáll from the pole, fear overcame him, and he started kicking and screaming and trying to drag his handlers toward the moors. The sheriff looked at Ubbi and shook his head before stabbing his sword through Njáll's back. He was dead before he hit the ground.

Ubbi prayed he'd be next. He prayed they'd have mercy

on Ve, who really shouldn't have even been there. None of them should've, but the others understood the risk. Ve was a follower, a simple stable boy who didn't want to miss out.

"Mercy!" Ubbi begged when they cut Ve from the pole.

The wiry Pict with the scratchy, now bloody beard, craned Ubbi's face toward the sheriff again and put his boot on the side of Ubbi's head.

They wouldn't let him turn away.

Ubbi cursed and cringed as he watched the worst consequence of his failure.

Ve locked eyes with Ubbi, confused, as two old men pushed him in front of the sheriff, then down to his knees in the mud made by the blood of their friends. The salt of Ubbi's tears stoked the fires of his wounds.

The sheriff put the tip of his sword just below Ve's chest. *Didn't the fat weasel know how to end a life properly?*

"Be strong, Ve! Tell the boys to save me a place at Odin's table...I won't be far behind."

Ubbi tried to act strong, but he knew the Valkyries wouldn't come for Ve. Not for a stable boy who'd never wet a blade. Not even for him, who'd only claimed a handful of Pictish souls. But he had to say something. He had to. Empty encouragement was all he had to give.

The sloppy sheriff stared at Ubbi, and might have even feigned a smile, as he leaned on the hilt of his sword.

A sound of wind rushed from Ve's chest and his body slumped. Ubbi would never forget the look of shock on Ve's tear filled face, as if he couldn't believe he was actually going to die, and the sound of his wheezing.

The sheriff nodded to two old men, who picked Ve up and tossed him onto the pyre as if he were just another log. But he wasn't dead yet, his spirit was still in him. As Ve roasted and cried and whimpered for his mother, Ubbi's chest burned as if they'd stoked the fires of his soul.

When Ve finally gave up the ghost, something inside

Ubbi broke. These Picts would hear his anger, whether they understood him or not. At first, it came out as a prayer.

"Vidar! God of vengeance! Make them bleed!" He lurched back, raising the pole, knocking his scratchy handler to his back. "If I die without satisfaction, let Tor and Olaf raze this village." Ubbi directed his threats to the sheriff. "And I'll have my revenge when I find whatever's left of you in Hel!" As he wailed, he imagined the axes and swords cutting through these people, his imagination the only water to cool his burning soul.

The sheriff walked through the fire Ubbi was spewing, and as if he were no more than a barking dog, cracked him across the head.

# PRIDE AND ALCOHOL

"Do you see something blue on the bottom of my foot?" Olaf planted his heavy boot between Knútr and Hallstein, practically kicking them off the log where they sat.

"No," Knútr looked confused. "Why?"

"I thought I'd stepped on a Pict!"

Around the fire, Olaf entertained the warriors with stories of tiny little Picts, as if they were no more than blue painted leprechauns.

"But don't worry men, we did not come in vain. They're scrappy, and they'll swarm the Gaels for me like ants at a picnic."

Olaf was already acting like an arrogant young lord, even though his parents had been nothing but farmers. The closest thing to a weapon his father wielded was a hoe to fight back the weeds. There was nothing exceptional about the man, actually, 'cept he'd married a beauty and fathered a giant.

Tor's father was a Viking, at least. He'd taught them both more than Olaf's father ever had, other than how to keep the goats out of the turnips, and who would ever want to have to know that?

"We've got a raid to plan." Tor took the drinking horn from Olaf's hand.

"What's to plan?" Olaf looked pissed, from the beer or the interruption, it was hard to tell. "We row up the river in the morning and raid a tiny village for the Pict King. As a reward, he lets me lead his little, blue-faced army north.

Then we earn our glory by killing Gaels for old Ketill Flatnose, the bastard king of the Isles." Olaf grabbed his horn back from Tor. "Tomorrow's the easy part. Tonight, we drink."

When Tor heard Olaf slur those words he knew any strategy, beyond what to take for a hangover, would be up to him. Olaf's plans were always the same. Send the youngest, fasted man in to set some fires across town, then cut in before the preoccupied fools realized they were under attack.

That had been Tor's strategy first. It had worked so well that Olaf didn't think it was necessary to consider any other way. As long as Scone was small enough for them to take, it probably would again.

Tor made his way back to the horses to pick the brain of the illegitimate Prince, Orri. Maybe he'd let Ubbi know he'd be going on the raid tomorrow, too. He'd be setting fires. Ubbi'd like that. Tor swatted a black fly. "Blood sucker." He was acting like a general—planning the attack while *Jarl* Olaf made merry with the men.

*When exactly did I give up my place at Olaf's side to become his second?*

Tor threw stones at rocks along the opposite riverbank. A warm mist rose up from the currents to bathe the moors.

*Somebody has to make a sacrifice. One of us has to make sure these men survive our ambitions.*

Tor's mind raced.

It was best to raid before the morning sun, of course, but Olaf was already too drunk for that. The only thing that was going to wake him in the morning would be an urge to water the grass. And probably not even that. They'd be lucky to start upriver before noon.

That meant they'd be going in swords drawn and shields up, so Tor needed to find out everything he could about the village. He needed to talk to Orri.

It was best that Olaf wasn't with him, he reasoned. Olaf

was a tactician, not a strategist. All swords and spears. The most he'd contribute would be obscene jokes and worthless drivel about glory and Odin's favor.

Tor startled Leif and Thorbjorn. "Where's the Pict?" He scanned the shelter they'd thatched together out of sticks and peat. The field was empty too. "Where are the ponies?"

The boys acted like they'd lost their tongues until Tor put his hand to Ice Breaker's hilt. His way of getting men's attention.

The story spewed from Leif like water from a mountain spring—how Orri had convinced the others that they could easily be back before morning with the stone, without spilling an ounce of Pict or Viking blood.

"He has friends there," Thorbjorn said.

"The Pict," Leif added.

Thorbjorn punched him in the shoulder.

Tor grabbed one with each hand and nearly pulled them off their feet. "When did they leave?"

Leif looked at Thorbjorn and Thorbjorn looked up at the sky. "They should be back soon."

Tor clanked their heads together like cymbals. "When did they leave?"

The boys looked at each other, and again, in unison, they agreed. "Probably four, maybe six hours ago."

Tor looked at the sky, hoping to find whatever these idiots had been looking for. While he'd listened to Olaf dazzle their men with his worthless tales and outright lies, camp guards and stable boys had snuck off to earn their glory.

For a second, he allowed himself to be impressed. "I'm proud of you two for not neglecting your duties." In truth, he wanted to kill them both for not getting him as soon as the others started scheming.

He thought about what he and Olaf might've done. Tor put his head in his hands. Probably gone after the stone, just like Ubbi and Bjorn. *But that won't save them from a beating when I get my hands on them.*

As Tor made his way back to the ships, he thought about some of the stupid things he and Olaf used to do, back when they were tasked to guard the ships. He guessed he'd kept some of these boys out of the fight too long.

*****

"They what?" Olaf knocked over the burning log and kicked the coals, splashing the men with fire and embers. "They dare try to steal my glory?"

As if Olaf setting his foot on fire were akin to a battle cry, the drunk Vikings jumped up from their log benches, cheered, and threw their cups and horns into the fire.

Olaf finished his drink, wiped his mouth with the back of his hand, and belted his sword. Leaves fell from the surrounding trees as if shaken loose from his thunderous burp.

"I hope you're feeling strong, boys, because we're rowing upriver. Tonight!"

The drunks responded with hoots and howls, many stumbling to the fire to piss out whatever dared to stay burning.

Tor wiped the sweat from his brow, cursing the gods as he dug for his hatchet. There was no stopping it now. Olaf had called the men to arms, and they were too drunk, or too stupid, to object.

Tor grabbed the confused Wid, who was watering a great oak. "How far to the village?"

# LAST WORDS

Ubbi drifted back into consciousness. One of his eyes was stuck shut from swelling and dried blood, which he tasted every time he licked his parched lips. *Why am I still alive?* What torture were they preparing to award the last of the Viking spies?

The sheriff beat his knife on the chain holding Ubbi's left hand. The tedious *ping* clanged around in his head like a cymbal. *Stupid Pict is dulling a perfectly sharp blade, and if he isn't careful, he's going to cut one of my fingers off.*

It was surprising how his rattled mind wandered. Ubbi thought about his life. All the things he hadn't done. How much he *hated* Picts. How easily his sharp, new sword had cut its way through the people in the square. How close he had come to killing the sheriff.

A ping sent a shard singing into his lip. Ubbi's thoughts dissolved, and when he bit it out and spit it to the ground, he tasted blood—from his lip or his tongue he couldn't tell. The sheriff watched and smiled. Ubbi tried to make himself small. *He's dulling it on purpose.*

The smith held out a pair of tongs. The sheriff yelled angrily and shoved them toward Ubbi, then pointed to his mouth. The Smith shook his head and laid it on top of the pole next to Ubbi's ear.

The language barrier was no longer relevant. Ubbi knew what the sheriff was planning to do next. He lurched at the sheriff but only managed, with a crunch of his nose, to land painfully face first on the hard dirt floor of the square. It made no difference. Two men grabbed the pole, raised him back to his knees, and held on.

After some hand motions and some gibberish, two men made their way out of the crowd and put their half-empty pints of beer on the ground. With filthy hands that tasted like boiled fish, they tried to force his jaws apart. Ubbi clenched down on his teeth, refusing to let them succeed.

*Just kill me and get it over with.* Ubbi could see his sword across the square every time the flames of the bonfire withered or parted. If he could only reach it.

The fat one let go of his lips and punched him in the ribs. Ubbi's reluctant cry allowed the other man to pry a knife in between his teeth. Ubbi bit down, while at the same time pulling his tongue back away from the blade. He wasn't sure what he was trying to do.

Hold it?

Bite through it?

The fat man, the one with the worst breath, stood in front of him and twisted the knife, prying teeth apart. The sheriff stepped closer, the tongs dangerously hovering near Ubbi's mouth.

*No!* Ubbi's tongue ducked around his mouth, hiding from the probing grip of the tongs while avoiding the knife's sharp edge. Finally, a big Pict Ubbi hadn't seen before pulled on leather gloves he took off the smith's counter, put his fingers in Ubbi's mouth, and jerked it wide open. With a crack of Ubbi's jaw, he'd lost the fight.

"Ah-ahhhrr-ah!" He was screaming inside, but outwardly it was hardly a whimper. Pain seared through him as the sheriff caught his tongue.

The tongs crushed down.

Hands wrestled his head into submission. Pulling hair and ears, calloused palms smothered his painful, bloody cheeks. The big man pulled, stretching Ubbi's tongue until he was sure it'd be torn out by the roots like a garden weed.

## HOW UBBI LOST HIS TONGUE

With a spark, the sheriff smacked his seax against the chain one more time. Ubbi screamed inside as the dulled, chipped blade disappeared from view.

The rough edge did its work.

Ubbi's mouth filled with fire. A snag, then warm, tinny blood. He struggled to gag and cough to clear his throat as the Sherriff pulled and something came away from his face.

His tongue.

The brute prying his jaws apart let go.

The Sherriff held it high in the air as the Picts prodded at it, watching it wriggle like a dismembered snake. Ubbi struggled to keep from choking. The fiery nub of what they left of his tongue painfully searched the backs of his teeth as if looking for its tip. He vomited on the big man's boots, coating them with breakfast and blood.

Angry fists bore down on Ubbi until cheek tore from bone. The big Pict looked exhausted when his shiny, red hands finally fell to his side. Unmercifully, Ubbi was still conscious.

Without a tongue, he couldn't even spit, and strings of blood drained from his loose jaw. After the gagging stopped, he trapped his lips together to try to swallow, but it was no use, his mouth filled too fast.

After spending a lifetime at sea, he was going to drown in his own blood in the middle of a village square.

The thoughts that race through a dying man's head.

*Would the sea goddess, Rán, try to claim his soul?* It was every Norseman's nightmare to spend eternity shivering, cold and wet in her bed at the bottom of the sea. *Did she have the power to fetch his soul from here?*

The sheriff cleaned the rough blade's edge with Ubbi's shirt and walked it over to the table at the smith's forge, then led the men that still remained back into the hall.

But Ubbi wasn't dead, yet.

He began to fear the morning, when ravens and crows

might pick at him while he still yet breathed. He'd seen it happen. More than once Tor had sent the older boys, like Ubbi, Bjorn, and Haldor, out to collect the iron and silver off the bodies after a raid. He'd been as uncaring as the Picts who left him now.

Ubbi himself had pulled the rings off dead fingers in plain sight of the survivors. Often women and children would watch from behind cracked doors and drawn curtains to see their husbands, fathers, and sons desecrated one last time.

For years, memories of the moans of the living would wake Ubbi from his sleep. He felt sorry for the ones still alive. The birds mercilessly picked at their wounds as if they were already dead. It was a rare son who was brave enough to stand over his dying father to protect him from the birds while Vikings were still on the field.

Before going through a dead man's pockets, Tor had taught them to test the bodies for signs of life with the tip of a spear—just in case.

It seemed like a mercy to finish them off before the birds got to their eyes.

While the boys searched the dead, the older warriors searched the churches and houses for treasures left behind—sometimes hidden, sometimes hiding.

The wind shifted, choking Ubbi with smoke, and jarring him back to the present.

In his half-conscious haze, Ubbi prayed to Thor for sleep, his mind already filling with spiteful, vengeful dreams.

The Pict women had shuttled their children away from the square around the time the tongs came out. They'd better find a place to hide. Olaf and Tor would be bringing the crows for their husbands—then they'd be coming after them.

As he choked down a gulp of his own blood. A sharp pain ran from his tongue down his spine, like someone had stuffed a fiery ember in his mouth.

Even though it was warm by the dying fire, hairs on his arms stood on end.

He wasn't alone.

A figure emerged from the alley, creeping toward him, hiding inside the long shadows cast by the dying pyre. They had murdered all of his mates in front of his eyes.

*Orri?* No. It was the sheriff's son.

# SHIPS, AXES, HAMMERS, AND SWORDS

Two longships rowed silently upriver. The light of the moon reflected off the water and the faces of the men. They looked exhausted, as if it were the inconvenience of the raid that had robbed them of sleep instead of their skins of Pict wine and endless stories by the fire.

Some of the lazy buggers volunteered to stay behind, but Tor wanted everyone except young Leif and Thorbjorn. Tor directed those two to break camp and load the third ship. He wanted to be ready to sail as soon as they got back, in case the raid went awry. If he wasn't sleeping, nobody would.

Thanks to the glory-seeking boys, the Picts would likely be ready and waiting. There would be no surprise raid tonight.

From the first ship, Olaf raised his fist.

Tor held his up in response, and the men raised their oars, leaving the two dragon ships to drift.

Making his way to the fore of the ship, Tor climbed up for a better view until his feet were on the rails. Leaning hard against the dragon's neck, he could just see it—a reflection on the water. An orange serpent slithering toward them along the water's edge.

He had to hand it to Olaf. Even when his words were slurred by the drink, his senses were keener than any man he'd ever known.

"Is *that* your missing boys?" Wid smiled as if looking forward to getting some sleep.

Tor clapped a hand over the Pict's big mouth.

The men on both ships craned their necks to see.

"Ease to shore." Tor pulled the leather thong hanging around his throat. His soul's golden covering was cold as he slipped two fingers inside.

He bowed his head and murmured a prayer to Odin.

"Allfather, someday I will sit next to my father in your hall...but not tonight." He raised the golden ring to his lips and kissed it. "Let us have the victory, and you can have the souls."

He dropped the soul ring into his shirt and eased Ice Breaker, his father's sword, noiselessly from its sheath. This was part of his ritual, something his father taught him to do before every battle.

"Wid," he whispered, "you stay with the ship."

After they pulled the dragons to shore, mail-clad warriors grabbed their shields and drew their weapons. Olaf and many others carried a spear and belted their swords. To the Norse, spears were to a battle as oars to a ship. Hallstein carried a hammer, a brutal bludgeoner he took off the body of a Briton after Knútr cut the legs out from under his mount.

In honor of his father, Tor always carried Ice Breaker into battle, and he always had a hatchet on his hip. The latter capable of unsaddling an armored man from his horse at full gallop, and equally useful for breaking into houses or delimbing trees for the fire.

*Too much light.* They needed cover. Tor surveilled the way ahead as he led the men up shore toward the serpent of flames. *There!* At the bend in the river, he could just make out the silhouette of a large, downed tree. Enough cover for the lot of them. If they could make it there first, they could surprise whoever came before they saw the ships. *Who would be stupid enough to use torches on a night raid?*

Before Olaf's enormous paw landed on his shoulder, Tor could feel his ale scented breath on the back of his neck.

"What's the rush," Olaf sputtered.

"We need to get into the forest up there or we'll lose the surprise."

"Surprise? They can probably hear the men wheezing from here."

"The only one I hear is you, Olaf. Come on, you fat oaf, beat me to that tree and I won't tell the cook to put you on a diet."

Aside from Olaf's complaining, the crew moved as quietly as ships through still water. Two abreast and a spear's length between them. No weapons clacked shields. No iron touched iron. Only Olaf's breathing betrayed them now.

Tor led the men behind the downed tree, twenty paces inside the wood-line. The light of a crescent moon slithered along the river's edge and into the grasses on the opposite shore, but where they hid was shrouded in darkness.

As the yellow of torches drew closer, Tor had to remind himself to breathe.

It was a Pict army, their voices carrying over the water. Tor could just make out what they were saying.

"They've captured the boys," he whispered to Olaf.

The giant man scowled at the ground and shook his head.

"They don't know how many of us there are."

That was the last of Tor's translation. The Picts were too close. They outnumbered them—four to one.

Tor held up his fist. A sign for the men to stand down.

"Let them pass," Olaf burped under his breath. "We'll cut off their retreat."

The Picts were too close for him to object, but that was a

bad plan. By cutting the Picts off from their village, the Norse would be cut off from their ships.

They watched from the shadows as the Picts swung their torches toward the trees, squinting for signs of movement.

Blue painted faces stared right at them.

A bead of sweat trickled down Tor's brow to the tip of his nose. He dared not move, and to Olaf's drunken credit, neither did he.

To their detriment, the Picts knew their own land. They were nowhere near the coast, so they were nowhere near the Vikings and their ships. The Picts saw exactly what they expected to see. Nothing.

As the army passed, Tor listened to them hide their fear under superstition. The young ones tried to scare each other with tales of banshees and ghosts and dead men rising from the moors.

The older men were quieter, whispering stories of soulless Viking raiders, big as bears and twice as dangerous. Apparently, they thought Northmen spat blood from between rotten teeth and adorned themselves with horned helms and armor made of the skulls of women and children killed in their heathen raids.

Tor had to bury his face in his elbow to keep his laughter from giving them away. The thought of mead horns tied to the side of Olaf's helmet had snot bubbling out of his nose.

"Keep it together!" Olaf whispered too loudly.

Tor caught his breath and wiped the tears from his eyes.

One of the Picts, more stupid than brave, swung his torch in their direction.

The blue-faced man squinted and followed his light into the woods without friend or shield.

Tor's father used to say, "A curious man will find himself in the belly of a bear." Whether by bear or banshee or troll or Viking, this man was destined to die young.

*Not yet.* Tor looked past the idiot at the passing troupe. Just—a few—more.

As if the man could hear Tor's thoughts, he stopped, laid his torch sideways on the very tree they were hiding behind, pulled down his trou and relieved himself on its bark.

Just on the other side of the mast, they were close enough to watch the man's eyes cross from relief.

Tor held his fist up high, a signal for every man to hold their position. He hoped the Pict couldn't hear their shallow breaths, which to Tor sounded like a band of trumpeters warming up for a show.

As the last of the Picts marched by, Olaf lurched sideways and a branch snapped. The man looked up, and his eyes found Olaf's.

His slack jaw closed, and he fell back, scurrying toward his men.

Olaf's spear let the air out of his lungs before he could scream.

With only the sound of rushing leaves, the Northmen descended on the Picts.

One of Tor's men grabbed the torch off the tree and lobbed it into the middle of the march, the fire adding more confusion to their faltering ranks.

The first clash was of wooden shields rushing two rows of unsuspecting Picts into the river, taking almost a quarter of them out without even wetting a blade. Olaf jerked his spear from the urinator's chest, turned it sideways, and drove three rows into the drink by himself, cutting many more with the head of his spear along the way.

The unlucky Picts wearing mail flailed to keep from losing their feet—with the ones that did falling to the bottom of the river like so many stones.

It was a nightmare every Viking thought about when wearing mail on the ships. The fear of drowning was why they faithfully practiced freeing themselves from their iron ringed shirts every time they put them on while aboard, regardless of how close to shore or how shallow the water when they landed.

After driving his few into the water, Tor put Ice Breaker to the test, cleaving a lanky Pict off at the elbow before he dragged Knútr into the river.

Olaf thrust his spear point into a man, then swung him into two more, knocking them into the water like kubb pins. Tor rushed through the opening to challenge the next row.

The Picts seemed hesitant to use the dark wood to fan out and create a perimeter, which was lucky, because this allowed his men to only face one row at a time. Harold Yellow-Leg fell aside with a dagger in his neck, but even he drove an old warrior into the drink when he fell. Tor filled the gap, driving a fat one into his neighbors. The man had so much paint on his face he looked like a blueberry.

Once they were off their feet, Tor pushed past, ruining sword hands, and stabbing hearts as he went. It was a form he'd tried to instill into his men. If you got your foe off his feet, maim the hand first, then put some iron in his heart for good measure. There was nothing more dangerous than a dying warrior who could still hold a blade.

Hallstein ran back out of the wood-line to make another charge at their flanks. He drove an entire row of Picts into the river, only to lose his footing and disappear with them into the black water. The last of the thrashing ended only a few paces from shore.

Tor could see the ships. They were driving the Picts back.

By now it was clear that the weak and inexperienced were bringing up the rear — mostly farmers and boys who had more skills with rakes and hoes than the weapons they'd be carrying to their Heaven that night.

"Don't steal my glory!" Olaf laughed as he pushed past Tor. He'd lost his shield, wielding a sword in his right hand and half a broken spear in his left. He was a sight to behold, towering over the Picts like a god. From the way the Pict's parted before Tor, they hadn't seen anyone like him before, let alone a monster like Olaf.

Olaf used the river as a third weapon. Many of the Picts tripped over their neighbor to stay out of his way, only to find themselves flailing in the drink to keep from drowning. It was like spearing flounder at low tide.

"I want to see some more shields up here!" Tor shouted to his warriors. "Two slashes and a stab!" he yelled to the men crowding to his flanks. He cut two wrists and put his sword into one's back as if showing them how it was done. "Einar! You and Knútr drop back to cover the rear. If a Pict crawls out of that river, I don't want them earning their fame by sticking Vikings in the back."

# VENGEANCE OF A DISGRACED SON

The sheriff's son pulled a dagger out of his belt. The son would finish what the father had started.

This was it.

Ubbi wondered if he'd done enough to impress the Valkyries. A crow lit atop the hall. Surely a sign that Odin had seen. Maybe he'd earned his seat in Valhalla, after all.

But instead of cutting his throat, the boy went to work on the ropes.

Footsteps from behind. The boy looked up, whispered something in the Pictish tongue, and re-sheathed his knife. A sword—*Ubbi's sword*—was handed to the Pict.

Ubbi started praying.

*Odin, Allfather, find me worthy. I crave Heiðrún's mead, not the thirst of Hella's cup.*

"Wake up," Orri spoke in Norse. "I can't believe you're still alive."

Ubbi opened his mouth and thick, clotting blood splashed out on the lordling's feet. "Gnnngh!" Ubbi gnashed his teeth. Even half a spit hurt like Sutr's whip.

The disgusted Orri scraped his bloodied boot off with a stick from the dying fire. "We're going to get you out of here."

The sheriff's son drew the sword back and forth in long strokes. Ubbi was so relieved he was being freed he almost didn't mind the fact that they were dulling his blade. *I can sharpen it later.*

Why was the sheriff's son freeing him? Where had Orri been? Why was he wondering about questions he could never ask? Ubbi's mind shifted to revenge. How could he murder every last Pict in that village?

He thought of options.

"Oengus doesn't want Vikings, or my father, to lead any armies into war against Scone," said Orri. "No matter what happened here, my father needs to end up with the stone to put this feud to rest."

Ubbi wondered what the real reason was. Maybe he didn't think Orri could make it back to the ships with the stone by himself.

All this for a rock. Not the real one at that. But who could tell? Screw 'em. Worst case, they see it's a fake and come back to torture everyone in the village trying to find it. Ubbi burned inside as he looked on the corpses of his friends.

The sheriff's son spoke to Ubbi. Orri translated.

"Oengus wants you to know he's sorry your friends died, but they shouldn't have killed that priest. And there's no need to come back. We've got the stone. Look around. There's nothing more for Vikings, here."

As if vengeance was nothing.

He wanted to scream. To shout. But without his tongue he wouldn't be able to form the words. Only pain.

Just before the final cut, Ubbi broke the last of the strands and grabbed the sheriff's son by the wrist, twisting until he let go of his sword. Ubbi laid its blade to the boy's throat. *I should kill the both of you.* He willed Orri to understand.

"He just saved your life." Orri must've thought Ubbi was as dumb as he was mute. "Now, let 'im go before his father comes back. All one of us would have to do is cry out, and you'd be worse off than before."

Laughter bellowed from the hall. Ubbi jerked the boy

close. The tip of the sword shook, scratching a little blood trail below the boy's left ear. He knew the sheriff's son had helped him after the damage was done, but where was he when they were carving his face? Where was Orri when they were murdering Haldor, or Ve?

He just wanted to kill everyone…

Blood traced a crooked line down the sheriff's son's neck.

No. The next blood this blade draws will be the sheriffs. Ubbi shoved the boy into Orri. Let him witness what I do to his father with Tor and Olaf at my side.

A cough sent a lightning bolt of pain stabbing into his ribs. Ubbi wiped blood and spittle from his chin. His jaw was sore from the beating, and his cheeks throbbed in sync with whatever was left of his tongue. Everything hurt, but he could move well enough. All down his front, his clothes were stained and sticky with his blood.

Ubbi knew the smartest thing he could do now would be to get out of that town with Orri and the false stone in tow.

*Tor and Olaf will help me deal with the village later.*

Ubbi pulled out his soul ring and considered thanking the Allfather for helping him escape. Blood had soaked into its fissures and cracks, making his soul appear black in the moon's waning light.

He looked at the hall. The men inside were talking, still high from their conquest over stable boys, as if they'd defeated a Viking hoard. Ubbi's heart pounded in his chest like a stranger at the door.

They must have been waiting for the return of their warriors. Praying to their God that they too had thwarted the Viking's plans.

Maybe they had.

But there was still one Viking left.

# REAL WARRIORS LEAD

Only farm hands would bring up the rear.
Tor slapped a man toward the water with his shield, but the man tilted, spun, and threw his blade at Tor's sword arm. It was the first decent response he'd seen. Instead of cutting the next man, Tor retreated a step and brought iron to iron. Ice breaker rang when its flat side met the other's edge. Having knocked the dangerous tip aside, Tor drove Ice Breaker into the man's chest, driving the first real warrior he'd faced down to his knees. Throwing his boot onto the man's chest, Tor withdrew his red, frothy blade as if from a sheath.

After drowning half the farmers bringing up the rear, the battle had finally begun. From then on, every bloody step he carved toward the front of the blue-faced army was hard won.

Olaf had made himself the tip of the spear, cutting into the Pict lines like he was clearing a field of tall grass.

Vigarr, Saxi the Blunt, and Hallstein, apparently the Unsinkable, were tied to Olaf's hip. A formidable line of attack against any enemy. The Picts parted before Olaf as if he was a shark swimming into a school of fish.

Tor led the rest of his warriors into Olaf's wake. He yelled his orders as he raised his sword and thrust it into a Pict's neck. "Knútr and Einar, finish the wounded! —and the rest of you, shields to Olaf, now!"

The Picts began falling in behind Olaf and the men he'd led too far. A tide of blue faces converged on all sides, separating them from Tor and the rest of the crew.

"Olaf! Fall back!"

But it was too late. The Pictish warrior class had baited him in. Not one of them would stand a chance against Olaf, so they stacked the odds against him.

Tor slashed and bumped and stabbed his way forward, leading a second line that should have never needed forming.

Olaf and his damned glory. Never thinking—always wanting the lead.

Shields were slowing down their progress, but Tor's line was cutting through. Experience and training had finally replaced the haze of the drink. The men's iron seemed sharper now, better wielded than the blue-faced banshee shaggers that were too scared or too stupid to flank them from the forest.

After Tor cut across a big Pict's throat, he stepped on the choking man's head to see how Olaf was faring.

Olaf, Vigarr, Saxi, and Hallstein stood back-to-back, doing what they could to fend off the swarm. Olaf was trying his best to draw one into the circle so he could put a dent in their numbers.

"Drive 'em all the way to the ships!" Tor commanded. His ears rang with screams of pain and cries for help, Pict and Norse alike. Shields clashed and iron rang against iron until he thought he might lose his grip.

*Odin help us!* This could be it.

Tor's lungs ached, too exhausted to penetrate the sounds of battle. Anger welled up inside him.

The berserker within overruled the commander. Forgetting about his followers, Tor thrashed and cut and stabbed his way forward.

*Damn any man who can't keep up.*

His mind was single-minded, no more cutting of hands or stabbing of hearts. The men to the rear could clean up his mess.

Tor's shield was his wall, and Ice Breaker cut down

everything to his strong side. The fury had taken him deep into the fray, and this was a fitting way to die.

How had Olaf gotten so separated?

Tor cut his way in, slashing the backs out of the knees of the Picts boxing Olaf in.

Olaf stood high above his tormentors, and Tor could see that he wasn't faring well. He had cuts on his face, arms, and chest, and his tunic was smeared with blood. Vigarr and Saxi lay dead underfoot. Hallstein was doing his best to protect Olaf's back. But he too was red with blood and looked to be the next to fall.

Surprising the Picts antagonizing Olaf from the rear, Tor drove a few more into the river before taking his place on Olaf's left. This position let him lend his sword to the giant's attack while shielding his weaker side.

How could Olaf let them draw him in without a shield?

"Should've waited for me, you big oaf!"

Olaf fell against Tor, nearly taking them both to a watery grave. Tor pushed back. It was like trying to push a stubborn donkey into an empty stall. Somehow, he managed to prop Olaf up and not get run through until Olaf found his legs.

"Keep your feet, now." Tor hit Olaf with an elbow, hoping the jolt would help him focus, "You're too fat for me to carry out by myself."

Einar beheaded a man before taking his place at Tor's left. Knútr and Karl were already there, propping the giant Viking up and protecting his forest facing flank.

Viking shields poured in through the hole Tor made, and by sword and ax and hammer and shield it widened...widened until a shield wall formed.

"Get Olaf out of here!" By then, they'd gained the advantage and pushed the Picts back beyond the ships. There was no sign of Wid, but Tor imagined he was safe and low and out of sight. As their lines steadied, the fizzing adrenaline subsided. The berserker inside Tor

## HOW UBBI LOST HIS TONGUE

stood down, and the commander regained control.

"Watch your flanks! Tighten up that wall!" Tor barked orders to his men. "Ankles! Spear the ankles."

"Drive the bastards to the sea," Olaf called out.

Tor couldn't help but smile. The big oaf hadn't given up his spirit yet.

"Get him into the ship!" Tor handed Olaf off. "We'll bypass Scone for now. We need to get Olaf directly to Drest for help."

"Drest and his people have no love for Vikings." Wid popped his head up out of his hiding place on Tor's ship like a weasel caught raiding an eagle's nest. "Show up without that stone, or Orri, and none of us are likely to make it out of there alive."

"I forgot about Drest's son." Tor rubbed his forehead with a bloody palm.

"It'll be quicker to go to Scone from here." Wid tried to sound upbeat. "Besides, I think you just defeated their army. In and out with the stone, get the ponies, then I know a shortcut by land to Drest. His people will be tending to Olaf and the rest of the injured in no time."

"Collect the souls and make a pyre, first." This was one thing Olaf insisted on.

"We've no time—"

"You don't take chances with men's souls, Tor," Olaf reminded. "Who knows what the banshee's or whatever else plagues these lands would do with our dead." Olaf groaned as the men struggled to hoist him over the rail of his ship.

"We can take care of that after."

"Enough! You'll anger the gods and lose the respect of the men. If I die, just throw me on the fire with the rest of 'em.

Tor hated Olaf's rituals, but was glad to hear every complaint. "If you survive this, you big oaf, you'll have to promise to cut back on the Krumkake."

Tor collected their dead's soul rings for burial back in Norway, while the men piled the bodies on a pyre. It surprised him every time he could lift a man's soul. Olaf couldn't even do that if they were still alive.

As he promised Olaf, Tor gave him the pouch to hold. Olaf always had a morbid interest in holding other men's souls.

While the men burned the bodies, Olaf mumbled a prayer to the gods. It was the most solemn Tor had ever seen him, and he didn't like it. They needed to get moving.

Tor let the men pick the Pict's pockets, but made them leave *their* soul rings untouched. Some complained they could pocket the souls and melt off the gold or silver or iron gildings while guarding the ships at Scone.

"We don't want to raise the ire of the spirits in this place," Tor reminded. "Let their gods or faeries or whatever these Picts have promised their souls to fight for them after we're gone, but they're not haunting us for a pittance of slag."

The smoke from the pyre followed the river as if eerily leading the way. Tor couldn't tell which was worse, the rotting stench of the moors, or the lingering scent of the burning bodies of his men.

"If those boys got captured and we have to fight again in Scone to get that stone, I'll kill them myself," Hallstein grumbled. Being pissed was the only thing keeping them going.

Harold Yellow Leg was gone, and so was Vigarr. Hella's frost, was Saxi dead, too? The smoke was clearing, but the smell of burned hair and flesh lingered on. Tor scrubbed his nose with the back of his sleeve to try to clear away the scent.

He needed a drink. They all did. They needed to grieve, and they were tired. Tired of rowing. Tired of fighting. Tired from lack of sleep. The grieving would come later — it always did.

# HOW UBBI LOST HIS TONGUE

A crow croaked from the mast, as if enjoying their displeasure.

"Keep an eye to shore, men, in case we pass them walking the road." Time for Tor to distract the men with some optimism.

"I'd wager they're all dead," Wid announced, as if he could read the stars, but not the mood.

Tor put his hand to Ice Breaker's hilt, feeling the berserker inside returning. No one would miss one more dead Pict.

"Actually, Tor's probably right." Wid seemed to get smaller, if that was possible. "I'm sure they're fine. The men of Scone have always been an odd bunch. Known to take long walks at all hours of the night."

"How much further?" Apparently, Tor needed to change the subject to give Wid something else to run his mouth about.

*Damn you, Olaf. I told you partnering with Picts was a bad idea.*

Olaf was asleep. Snoring. But at least he was breathing.

"He'll survive," Tor muttered. "Probably just the drink."

Olaf emptied a skin of something one of the men stole off a dead Pict after they heaved him into the ship. Said it was for the pain.

*We should have never left Norway.*

# THE FIRST SHERIFFSON RAID

The crow cawed down from his perch as if the Allfather himself were mocking him. *Why would Odin ever welcome me into Valhalla?* Ubbi put his soul ring back in his shirt and stared at the hall. The Picts clacked like chickens, so loud he could hear them from the square. He imagined them telling stories of their glorious victory and laughing with the sheriff about how he'd taken the Viking's tongue.

"We need to go now."

Ubbi shook Orri's hand off his shoulder.

"Aannngh!" Ubbi trembled after thoughtlessly wiping the sweat from his brow. The agony of scraping the back of his hand against his wounds momentarily took his attention away from his tongue. "Mmmph!" His teeth gnashed. *Can I not express my own pain, even muted, without it feeling like licking shards of glass?*

A new anger lit inside. If their army burned the ships, he would die here anyway — by the torture of these blue-faced demons or by drowning in their moors or by one of their banshees screams.

Visions of Olaf and Tor swinging from a tree near the mouth of the river flashed in his mind. A warning to Northmen to do their raiding elsewhere.

Ubbi stared up at the mocking crow — blacker than night — and held his sword up in defiance, angry at Odin for making him take his revenge in such a weakened state.

*Tell your master to send the Valkyries for Ubbi the Tongueless. For I will earn my seat in his hall, tonight.*

## HOW UBBI LOST HIS TONGUE

Ubbi's anger burned hotter against Odin than the sheriff, but there was a gift in it. He felt power in the clarity of knowing he would die soon, and he was ready.

"Nggh!" A fresh pain woke Ubbi from his thoughts. He'd been sawing at the rope binding his other hand and had foolishly cut into his wrist.

"Mind the blade!" Orri's eyes widened with fright. "You can't afford to lose any more blood. You look a pint low already."

Ubbi grabbed his sword by the blade, and with a quick stroke, he swung the handle into the sheriff's son's head, putting the unsuspecting boy on the ground.

"What are you doing?!" Orri raised his hands and backed away as Ubbi flipped the sword and aimed the sharp end at his face. Ubbi recognized the look of a coward. King Drest had raised his bastard son to be a politician, not a warrior. All mouth and no action. The kind that wouldn't last a week at the oar on open sea. The kind Tor would put in charge of the dogs.

Ubbi sheathed his sword, grabbed a fiery branch off the fire, and used the light to rummage around the smith's booth until he found a few long pieces of iron.

He pushed the flaming branch into Orri's hand, grabbed a hammer off the table, and led the useless prince to the hall.

He held up his hand and put four bloody fingers over Orri's mouth. When he let go, there were red stripes atop the half-Pict's pink lips. *Good.* No reason he should be the only one with blood on his face. He lifted the first piece of iron up and slid it through the door's handles. It went through without the need of the hammer. Maybe his luck had changed.

Orri silently mouthed the words, "What are you doing?" and motioned in the direction of the ponies.

Ubbi shook his head and pointed the piece of iron toward the back. When they arrived, he handed it to Orri and pointed at the handles.

Orri lowered his eyes and shook his head in defeat as he slid the second piece of iron through to lock the back door.

*It's your fault we're here, and you will have blood on your hands.* Ubbi wished Orri could hear what he was thinking, but from the look on Orri's face, he guessed he understood.

Ubbi dragged Orri by the shirt to the woodpile just outside the back door. The two of them piled dry, quartered pieces of wood high along the back wall.

Orri dropped three logs, as if they were just two boys making a campfire behind their father's house. Ubbi glared at the boy drenched in sweat.

After the fire took, Ubbi had Orri fill his arms with wood and the two made their way back to the front door.

A man was rattling the door from the inside, but the iron lock held it shut. He sounded confused, and there was laughter. They still didn't realize that the building was burning on the other side.

*Stupid Picts.*

Ubbi dropped his wood against the door and knocked Orri's out of his hands. *Their God will have to sift through ashes to collect these souls.*

Fire climbed up the outside wall until it licked at the eave overhead.

Panic replaced the festive sounds inside as the Picts realized what was happening. It sounded like they were slamming everything they had against that front door, including the benches. To the builder's credit, it held strong.

"We need to run." Orri pulled Ubbi's shirt. Dried blood ripped scabs off his wounds. Ubbi would've yelped had crying out not felt like licking hot coals. Instead, he grabbed the smith's hammer with one hand, and Orri's arm with the other.

## HOW UBBI LOST HIS TONGUE

Orri cowered like a boy who'd seen beatings before. These Pict fathers must've been terrible.

Ubbi pushed the smith's hammer into his hand. He wanted to be ready to kill as many as they could if that door gave way.

While they waited, Ubbi warmed his hands by the fire and reveled in the screams. It was the melody of revenge, and to Ubbi, it was the most pleasant the Pictish tongue had ever sounded.

*****

By the time Tor showed up, Ubbi and Orri were sitting next to the pyre in the middle of Scone's square. Orri'd urged him to leave, but Ubbi refused. He figured he'd rather the Valkyries find him among his handiwork rather than at the bottom of some Pict bog on the way back to the ships. Whether Orri stayed because it scared him to go back alone or whether he was protecting Oengus, he didn't say. But he stayed, and Ubbi was glad he did.

When Ubbi saw Tor leading that small band of men into Scone's square, swords drawn and jaws open, he suffered to wipe the burning salt of tears from the cuts on his cheeks. Then, as if receiving unexpected guests, he jumped to his feet, straightened his shirt, sheathed his sword, and threw another log on the pyre. Scabs popped painfully across his face as he failed to hold back a smile of relief.

Ubbi noticed his decoration had tilted, so he pulled back the hair to straighten the charred, tongueless head of the sheriff he'd staked on a pike like a totem.

As his last act before leaving for the ships, Ubbi pulled the gag out of the sheriff's son's mouth, cut his bonds, and handed him his father's sword. It was as blackened as his father's head. After receiving his freedom, the boy stared at Ubbi, then Tor and the others, and trudged up the road toward his house. He was unharmed except for a cut on his neck and a knot on his head from the pommel of Ubbi's newly broken in sword.

# DELIVERING THE STONE

There was no time.
Orri would have to explain what happened on the way. The boy was alive, and he'd captured the stone for his father. That was enough. They'd have to weigh the cost later. Right now, Tor needed to focus on getting Olaf and Ubbi and the rest of the injured to Drest's healers.

He'd have to decide if he still wanted his army later.

The crew had recovered the ponies, which they needed because the river Tay had taken the ships as close to Drest as it could.

"Find some carts for the injured, and as many more horses as you can find. But no looting. We need to be on our way before the sun rises."

It was only when they loaded Olaf off the ship that Tor saw the extent of his injuries. Shallow stabs pocked his body with blood and left him pale. There were so many wounds, it was like he had stepped on a bee's nest. No one Pict could take Olaf alone, but together they'd picked him apart. But his reach was long, and he'd left a wake of bodies of those that dared get too close. Live or die, stories would be told of what Olaf had done that night.

"Easy with Olaf, men." Tor had them move the wounded into carts, including Ubbi, the only one of the Norse boys to survive. Four more souls to add to Olaf's pouch of rings.

Tor left six healthy men to guard the ships and followed

Wid the trader into the moors. Orri told him all about what had happened, from when Tor left him with the stable boys to what happened in Scone. The boy had a talent for storytelling. Somehow, he managed to make Ubbi's stupidity sound heroic, while building a case for rescuing him and his mother from Drest. It was all so ridiculous, but entertaining enough to pass the time. Tor looked back at Ubbi, scabbed and sleeping soundly in the cart. Orri's was the only version of the story he'd ever hear.

"See, I told you I knew a shortcut. Not too much further, now, is it Orri?" Wid looked as proud of himself as if he'd cut the trail through the moors himself.

"Just the other side of those trees." Orri pointed in the distance.

Tor was glad for any direction at this point. Since they'd left the river, he'd gotten turned around somehow. With all the twists and turns they took around the stinking bogs before the sun came up, and with only a few stands of forest to anchor to, he was as lost as a whore in a convent.

"Good, these moors stink of rot." It was the most positive thing Einar had said since they'd left the ships.

"More like death," said Orri. "It's worse in the heat of summer. Even people who've been here their entire lives can go missing in the moors."

"Shut it," Hallstein groaned. As one of the injured, Hallstein rode a pony, but Tor considered making him walk if he didn't suck it up.

Orri spoke louder. "The moors 'ave ended many a man and beast. Even the dead have been said to lose their way, here."

"What's the boy talking about, Wid?" Einar craned his neck so far back that his neck cracked.

Wid shrugged. "Lost people who've managed to find their way home say they saw strange lights hovering in the moors. Thinking they might get some help, they follow 'em, only to find themselves more turned around than when they started."

"I think I saw some of those earlier." Hallstein's voice quivered.

At least he'd stopped his moaning.

"'Tis Stingy Jack and his lantern, leading the lost off the path." Orri didn't seem happy that Wid was trying to tell his tale. "Jack's hoping if he collects enough souls that he can buy his way into heaven."

"Stingy Jack?"

Did Einar wipe a tear from his eye? Tor couldn't keep from looking over his shoulder. Well, anything to entertain the men.

"Jack was a swindler, through and through. They say he was a smith by trade, and he never charged a copper if he thought he could get two."

"Must be related to Einar," Hallstein said, at least enjoying the distraction.

"Well, Stingy Jack had a visit from the Devil, come to collect his soul for his evil ways."

"Evil?" gruffed Einar. "This man was no relative of mine."

He'd heard about the Christian hell and must not have liked the sound of where this was going.

"Just let 'im tell the story." Hallstein started coughing and moaning until someone passed him a skin of mead.

Wid raised an eyebrow high at Einar. "Shall I finish, then?"

"Well, old Jack was as clever as his soul was black, and he convinced the Devil to turn himself into a copper so he could buy one last drink before he go." Wid scowled at Einar, shutting him up before he interrupted again. "Once the Devil turned, old Jack put the coin in his pocket next to a crucifix he'd swindled from a drunken priest. Well, as you may know, the Devil's powerless against the cross. So he was locked in old Jack's pocket until he promised he wouldn't take his soul to Hell."

"But you're skipping the best part," Orri interrupted.

"The town is right up, there, boy. I think they've heard enough of it to get the point.

"Well," Orri said, not about to give up his chance to run his mouth a bit, "Stingy Jack, as clever as he was, may have won the battle but still lost the war. Cause Saint Peter wasn't about to open the gates of Heaven for an unrepentant sot like Jack. So, Jack had no choice but to go back to the Devil, hat in hand, and ask if he would give 'im a room in Hell. Well, the Devil refused out of spite, but since he appreciated a lying trickster as much as any demon, out of respect for having outwitted him, the Devil gave Jack an ember from Hell's own fire—something to light his way as he wandered the twilight world, lost for all eternity. My father says it's because the Devil wanted to know where he was so he could avoid ever having to see him again." Orri waited, as if Tor would appreciate his father's cleverness. He didn't. Unsatisfied with the silence, Orri kept on. "Well, clever Jack carved a turnip to make a lantern to carry his light. And to this day, he wanders the moors, using Hell's fire to lure Christians off the narrow path to drown in the bog so he can collect their souls, in hopes to use them to barter his way into heaven."

"Shut up with all that." Einar fell back to the rear and didn't talk to Orri again.

"He ought to take his lantern back toward the ships, then." Hallstein perked up. "He'll find a lot of Christian souls back there."

"Hallstein!" Tor barked. "Shut up and check on Einar."

Tor shook his head as Hallstein complained his way to the back of the line. *Idiot thinks bragging about killing Picts in front of their king's son's a good idea.*

*\*\*\*\*\**

Their arrival was not a welcome one. This many

Vikings rarely was.

"Tell my father we have the stone." Orri sat up straight as they stopped at the guard outside the hall.

"And we have his son." Tor pushed Orri back in his seat. "We need healers. We have many injured men that need attention."

Tor gave the reins to one of the crew who'd been walking and dismounted along with Orri and Wid.

Time to be diplomatic.

The old witch came out first, soon followed by Orri's mother. The boy's face turned red when she hugged him. She scowled at Tor when her hand ran into the tight grip he held on the back of Orri's shirt.

The old witch scrunched up her nose at the sight of the men laid out in the cart. Her brows raised when she saw Olaf there, pocked with stains of dried blood. She sniffed the air about him, then moved on. She spat toward Wid, then walked a circle around Tor and Orri. Tor hated witches—always bold when anyone else would be fearful.

She stopped in front of Orri, smiled a toothless grin, and spat, again. "Give the stone to me, son. I need to see if it's authentic."

"Not until my men are cared for." Tor pulled Orri back, away from the hag.

The crone hissed, then smiled and backed away. "Lay these men on the ground in the tree's shade, where we can attend to them."

Three girls dressed in black appeared from a gathering crowd and led the carts and injured men under the sprawling limbs of an old, twisted elder tree.

"Aislin," the witch called, and a pale, brown-haired girl with the biggest brown eyes Tor had ever seen appeared at her side.

Tor glanced around to try to figure out where all these girls were coming from.

"Aislin, dear." The hag put a small sack in the girl's

hand. "Just a pinch in a cup of beer. No more." The woman stopped her again. "Maybe two for the giant. Wet some cloth to cover the cuts on the boy's face."

A company of armed Picts poured out of the hall, blue still drying on their faces, like girls who'd just finished making themselves up for a dance.

The last of them was King Drest. This time there was no blending in with his people. He had a thick blue stripe drawn cleanly across the top of his face, was wearing a Pictish skirt, and a sword dangled low on his hip. He looked underfed, which was as common among Picts as their love of makeup.

Tor couldn't help but wonder where they got a color like that. *Could it be something in the soil?* Other than Pict faces, he'd only seen it on fish and crabs.

"You come armed and in force, stained in the blood of my people," Drest said. "Where is your Jarl?"

"King Drest." Tor lowered his head, but not his eyes. There were too many weapons for this greeting, and an unreasonable show of force. His hand found the hilt of his sword, which was a habit he meant to break, but only realized he was doing it after his fingers found the pommel.

A black crow flitted between them toward the injured. *Never a good sign.*

"Your healers are tending to Olaf's injuries. I speak for us." Tor was no Olaf, but if it was height the King respected, he was still two heads taller than any Pict, and half as much taller than most Vikings he'd ever met. "We have your stone, but it came at significant cost."

"Well, if my army is to help you push the Gaels out of the Northern Isles, then I think you'll find it a bargain."

"We're tired, boy," Tor whispered in Orri's ear. "Give your father the stone so he'll dismiss these men. Then we can get something to eat and some much-needed sleep."

The witch leaned forward when Orri held out the stone.

## HOW UBBI LOST HIS TONGUE

Tor kept his grip firm on the boy's shirt. Orri was the only insurance they had to keep from being overrun.

The Picts were like ants, small but relentless. Every man, woman, and child, blue-faced or not, carried a blade and knew how to use it. Even if they lost ten for every Northman, they'd make quick work of what was left of Tor's crew if Drest so much as touched the hilt of his sword.

The old crone eased the stone from Orri's palm.

"Give it to me." The king held out his hand. The old witch's eyes seemed to shift colors as she examined it.

"Where'd you get this?" The woman reached out to Orri, but Tor jerked him back—for his own sake or Orri's, he wasn't sure.

Drest grabbed the woman by the cloak, "I said, give it to me!"

Tor thought he heard her hiss when she turned. Drest released his grip. The woman wiped the spittle that dribbled onto the back of her hand onto her shirt, grabbed the King by the wrist, and dropped the stone into the palm of his hand.

"Ubbi found it in the church,' Orri explained. "It was set in a gold frame, sewn into a tapestry hanging on the wall."

"I need to see the frame," the old woman snarled.

Orri mumbled something under his breath.

"Speak up." The queen rolled her eyes at her husband's bastard.

Orri's mother hung her head. She had lost her place in the front by the crowd that had now filled the square in front of the hall. There were blue faces everywhere, and Tor was wondering if he shouldn't send a man to check on Olaf. He twisted his grip on Orri's shirt and whispered in his ear. "Give them what they want, boy."

Orri turned around. "Ubbi kept it."

Tor's head fell back out of habit, as if asking the gods

for a break. His neck cracked when he rolled it back and forth.

"Einar, go get Ubbi," he said, then lowered his voice. "And check on Olaf while you're at it. Tell him I could use his help if he's able."

# KEY TO THE KINGDOM

Einar dragged a loopy Ubbi over next to Orri. Bloody bandages crisscrossed his face. The sea of Pict faces cringed at the sight of him.

"Are you the one who found the stone?" King Drest asked.

Tor translated.

Ubbi nodded.

"And there was a gold frame?"

Ubbi reached into his pocket and drew out a little piece of cloth. Stitched in its center was a gold star, cut on one side where he'd pried the stone free.

A guard snatched the cloth out of Ubbi's fingers and handed it to the King. Drest tried to line the stone up with the frame.

"This is useless. The thieving Viking ruined it."

Ubbi looked as if he was having a hard time keeping his eyes open. He reached into his belt, unhooked a skin, and offered it to Tor.

Tor pushed it away. "Mind the king, Ubbi. I didn't wake you because I was thirsty."

"Tell me," said the witch. "Describe the image stitched into the cloth from where the stone was taken."

Ubbi shrugged his shoulders.

Orri started. "It was—"

"Let him speak!" the queen screeched.

Everyone looked away from her except Orri's mother, who stared a hole in the back of the woman's head. "Stop putting words in his mouth."

The king just shook his head. "Somebody, other than Orri, translate for the boy."

"That won't help." Orri ignored the queen as if appealing to his father for support.

"And why is that?" The king seemed frustrated for witnessing his own family's dysfunction.

"It won't help, because the sheriff took his tongue." Orri smirked as if he enjoyed exposing the queen for a fool.

"I see." The king fiddled with the stone in his palm, as if just realizing that it probably cost the souls of every man, woman, and child in Scone.

The priest at the king's side started praying, and whispers and gasps flowed through the crowd like a ripple in a pond.

Tor tightened his grasp on Orri's shirt and shifted to the side to hide the fact that he was again sliding his hand down to the handle of his sword. Only this time he knew he was doing it.

"Why can't you just try it?" asked Orri.

Tor loosed his grip mid-sentence so the boy wouldn't sound like he was being strangled by the collar of his shirt.

"Try it?" asked the king.

"That's much too dangerous," said the witch. "Give it to me, sire. I'll try it for you." She reached out to him with her twisted fingers.

As if horrified at the notion, Drest pulled the stone in tight to his chest. Two guards stepped in to block her advance.

The woman bowed but kept her wrinkled paw out. "I just want to ensure it is safe, my lord. If it works, I will give it back to you. I promise."

"What is happening?" Tor whispered to Orri in Norse.

"They say David used the stone to kill the giant, Goliath."

Tor didn't understand what this boy was talking about.

## HOW UBBI LOST HIS TONGUE

"It's a story from the Bible." Orri slipped back into Pictish.

"You Christians...You call our stories myths, but there are giants in your Bible, too. You want us to destroy our idols, but then you worship sticks and stones."

"They're not sticks," said the old crone. "They're crosses. And we don't worship the stone. It's a key."

Tor ignored the hypocrisy. "We have witches, you have witches."

"That woman is a nun of the church!" The queen's jaw tensed.

Tor shifted Orri between himself and the witch like a human shield. "Sorry, lady, but I can't tell the difference."

"Sister!" The king was talking to the witch, but he looked at Tor as if he'd just tracked dung into the hall. "Just tell me what I need to do."

"Will one of the Picts stab their king in the back and get it over with?" Olaf whispered to Tor in Norse.

Tor's heart missed a beat. Olaf had never snuck up on anyone in his entire life.

"Well, isn't that how the Picts gain the throne?" Olaf smiled. He was shirtless. His wounds were dressed, and color had returned to his face. He looked better. Too much better.

Tor smiled at the sight of the big oaf. "The Pict healers must know magic. You look like you visited Valhalla, shared a beer with Odin, and convinced him to let you come back to see the nun's trick."

"Heh," Olaf chortled. "Those hens were worthless. All they did was peck at my wounds and pray—keeping me company, until the crows showed up." Olaf stared at king Drest when he said it.

"Maybe they can save the next one." A tall, bearded man leaning on a staff seemed to appear out of nowhere.

This time, Tor choked Orri when he jumped. Maybe he needed a healer to see what they could do for his eyesight too.

"Who are you, stranger? I'd like to know who to thank for helping our special guest." Drest didn't look pleased with any of this.

The man was old, but not crooked, and stood almost as tall as Tor. He was dressed in gray from his cloak to his hat. There was something familiar about him, but Tor couldn't put his finger on it. He was obviously no Pict.

Ubbi tried to push his wineskin into Olaf's hand.

Olaf grabbed him by the collar. "Don't you have horses to water, priest?" Olaf shoved the skin into Ubbi's chest, knocking him to the ground. "Now back off. I don't want you blowing this for me, like you did in Scone."

Ubbi lowered his head, put the skin back on his belt, and faded back a step like a kicked dog.

Tor stared up at Olaf. *What got into him?* He wished he felt as fresh as Olaf looked. Made sense, though. He hadn't slept in two days and Olaf had been resting since they left the ships.

Tor looked at the wanderer again. *Hadn't he been taller? And leaner?* It was like he'd changed before his eyes. Like a dream he couldn't recall except for the feeling it left behind. Tor hated that feeling, like when he misplaced his knife. It was like he was turning into his father.

"Great King." The queen lost her regal poise and seemed to salivate. "We can talk to strangers over dinner... There are more pressing concerns at hand."

It was a joke among the Vikings that Pict kings die young and with knives in their backs. And it was looking more and more like Drest's demise would be coming from his queen.

# CROSSING INTO FAE

"This is a power only the king should command." Drest stood up as straight as his crooked bones would allow. He wasn't that old, just spindly. Something most Picts had in common. Not enough branches on the tree, is what Tor's father used to say.

"Remove your soul, my King," the nun said.

Drest pulled an iron chain from inside his shirt. His soul matched the chain, covered in iron, unpolished and plain.

Ubbi looked angry, but seemed to have gotten his legs, even pulling his own soul ring out from his shirt and following along.

"Now, put it in your palm, and drop the stone into the middle of the ring." The nun licked her thin lips. "Give him some room." The nun was salivating over what was in the king's hand. "It's been lifetimes since anyone has used the keystone to cross to the other side."

The crowd backed away from their king.

Ubbi leaned closer.

Drest looked nervous as he held the stone over his soul. Its iron plate caught the morning sun, reflecting a silver light from the palm of his hand.

"This is ridiculous," Tor whispered to himself. He didn't remember letting Orri go, but his hand had left the boy's shirt and was now holding his own gold-plated soul. The braided leather thong that held it around his neck was worn and fraying.

Better get that replaced before it's lost.

Tor thought about how worn his soul looked the day

the priest cut it from his chest, mottled and cracked, not too different from Ubbi's. If the boy survived, and they got the Pict Army, he'd make sure he got enough silver to get it covered.

Maybe the king and his nun were about to show them the soul ring's purpose.

Ubbi mirrored the actions of the king. By now almost everyone was holding their rings, except Olaf and the stranger.

The stranger had changed again, somehow. Maybe Tor had gotten hit on the head in the battle by the river. *Wait, his cloak was gray before, wasn't it?*

King Drest held the stone over the ring lying in his palm as he finished a silent prayer to his god.

"Amen."

Then he dropped the stone into it and lifted the ring up, allowing the stone to pass through.

Tor looked at the nun, then back at the king. Nothing. *What was all this anyway?*

The stranger smiled and watched as Ubbi mimicked the king, raising and lowering his ring from his palm. Only he had no stone. Maybe he needed the stranger's healing, too. Ubbi's dressings were caked with dried blood, while Olaf's were clean.

"What is going on, here?!" the king shouted at Orri. "Are you sure this is the stone?"

Olaf stepped into the king's path. Drest stumbled aside to avoid him, and several of his men caught him before he fell. Drest looked incensed but did not draw his sword.

"*He* has it!"

Did the king not see how weak this all made him look? If no one's seen this stone's magic before, why not just lie and say it worked? He could always kill the nun later and nobody would be the wiser.

"Ubbi?" the stranger asked.

How did he know Ubbi's name?

"Did you steal the stone?"

Ubbi stared at the stranger's eyes, sharp and piercing. He shook his head.

"Why not ask your son." Olaf pushed Orri forward into the midst of the Picts, who seemed to be closing in from all sides since the king's magic trick failed.

A taller, stronger looking Pict with a blue handprint drug across his eyes whispered into Drest's ear. He wore two blades. A knife completely forged of iron, hilt to tip, hung in a leather baldric strapped across his naked chest. A short sword sheathed on his left hip, the leather wrap on its hilt worn thin from use.

The king shook his head.

*Stupid oaf.* Tor tried to will Olaf to understand. Orri was their hostage. The hilt of Tor's sword was still damp with blood from the last battle. Things felt like they were going against them again.

"Orri? Did you see Ubbi remove the stone?" Tor asked in the Pictish tongue so the king would understand. Although, at this point Tor had the feeling Drest understood Norse all along.

Orri looked at Ubbi, then up at the stranger. "I saw him pull the stone from the cloth. The only thing he took was the frame."

"And the head of the sheriff." Olaf laughed.

The king whispered something to the Pict with the iron knife, and the man slipped back into the increasingly dense crowd.

Tor shook his head, hoping Olaf would just shut his mouth. *What had gotten into him?*

"What was the Viking doing with the stone in the first place, Orri?" The queen curled back her lips in a sneer. "You should've never let him handle it."

Drest held his soul in his fingers and dropped the pebble through again.

Nothing happened.

"This isn't it."

"Well, it's not much, I'll say," Olaf laughed. "Tor, tell the king we need some food and a place to rest. Then we need to plan to journey north. I don't know if these Picts march or run or ride. But I'll allow King Drest to sail with us if he'd like." Olaf took a drink from a red flask that Tor had never seen before.

*He'll allow? What has gotten into him?*

"You have embarrassed the king." The queen stepped forward. The king tried to stop her with a hard look, but controlling that woman must've been like trying to skin a live eel. "In front of our people and our Lord, they have made you look like a fool! As did her son." She turned back to scowl at Orri's mother.

"You are the only one embarrassing me." The king stepped in front of his wife and found himself within arm's reach of Olaf.

Olaf smiled down at him.

"I-I-I am a Christian—so I will show you grace." He backed up slowly, leaving his stubborn queen to stand alone. She shook her head like a disappointed mother and turned to join him in his retreat.

Iron Knife returned and whispered something in King Drest's ear.

"You came here asking for an alliance, and all you gave me in return was the blood of my people." It was never good to embarrass a king. "Now pack up your injured, leave my kingdom, and keep your ships north of the Scurdie Ness."

Tor looked at the faces in the crowd. The Picts not wearing blue paint were biting their lips, gazes averted. The politicians and traders who were expecting to profit from the alliance disappeared behind closed doors so fast it was like water leaving the fjord at low tide.

Drest's army filled in the gaps. They seemed emboldened, and Tor guessed why. Better to fight a handful of Vikings already broken by the ghosts of Scone than die in the Northern Isles in a political war.

"Father." Orri broke the silence. "Wouldn't it be better to join the Northmen to push back the Gaels in the Northern Isles rather than wait for either of them to come south?"

"You deserve this." The queen said it to her husband as if this were the time. "You've kept that Norse woman around as your prize, and now your bastard wants Picts to die fighting for her people. These men just murdered our brothers and sisters in Scone. They've stolen the stone of David. I can't believe you ever considered an alliance with Vikings in the first place."

Tor never understood how these powerful men could rule a nation, and yet could not control their own wives.

The queen continued. "You run one settlement of Vikings off a stolen farm and because you kept one for a pet, you think you're able to bargain with these… heathens."

"Olaf?" Tor whispered. "Can you fight?"

Olaf smiled and looked down at his hand. He was leaning on the hilt of a great axe.

"Einar," Tor said. "Take Ubbi and the rest of the injured to the carts.

Olaf grabbed him before he left. "And grab some of those girls tending the wounds, if you can." Einar looked at Olaf like his sail was stuck at half-mast. "Oh, and be sure to take their terrible medicines too."

Einar grabbed Ubbi's arm, and they slipped back into the crowd.

"What's wrong with you, Olaf? This isn't a raid. We'll be lucky if he lets us leave here alive." Tor was glad to see the few healthy crew had drawn close since the queen's rant, shields and swords in hand.

Olaf grabbed Wid by the arm and pulled him out of his shadow. "Time to earn your keep, Pict. Convince your king to honor his word or Vikings will plague this land 'til Ragnarök comes."

Wid's mouth puckered in confusion, either at the end times reference or that he'd so easily been made to piss himself. It was hard to tell.

Tor grabbed Orri by the arm and pulled him back. Two human shields in a sea of Picts.

"Lord Drest." Orri's mother fell at his feet. "They have our son."

The king helped her up.

"Stupid slave," the queen chortled. "Don't you remember who gave *your son* to them in the first place?"

King Drest looked sternly at the queen, then spoke gently to Orri's mother. "It's better this way." Then he spoke to Olaf in perfect Norse. "Take the boy and go back to your ships. If you haven't set sail by nightfall, I'll have my men strip you of your weapons and have the women cut off your balls and hang them wherever the sheriff put the boy's tongue. We'll see if your Valkyries think you are worthy of Valhalla, then. Now, who has the stone?" King Drest tossed the worthless stone in the air.

"Your son says you do, King." Tor locked eyes with Drest.

"Orri, this is the last chance, son. Who has the real stone? Maybe your tongueless friend?"

Orri looked around, but Tor had sent Ubbi to get the injured. Then he did the most surprising thing of all. "You have it, father."

"We'll have to search the bodies then." King Drest exhaled, staring through his son. "Kill them all, for the theft of the Stone of David and the murder of the innocents of Scone."

# TRICKS OF THE RAID

Tor pulled Orri back and put his knife to his throat.
"No!" his mother screamed.
Tor leaned back against his men. "Looks like Odin wants to drink with us tonight, boys. Do what you can to make him wait."
The tall stranger smiled, and something about his gaze made the hair raise up on the back of Tor's neck. The stranger whispered in Olaf's ear.
As if in a battle rage, Olaf drew back his axe.
"Olaf, no!" Tor tried to grab his arm, but it was too late.
The cleaver sung, relieving two Pict necks of their burden. Painted heads flew. A face slapped into the queen's chest, staining her dress crimson and her bosom with a blue frown.
The Picts not smart enough to run from Olaf looked confused as their heads left their shoulders.
"Kill them!" the queen screeched. "Kill them all!"
Tor leaned hard against his men.
A Pict stabbed at Orri with a dagger, but Tor turned his knife against him and stabbed him in the neck, dropping him at Orri's feet.
Tor plucked the bloody instrument and handed it to Orri.
"Live as a Viking or die as a Pict. Make your choice, boy." Tor drew his sword in one hand and his hatchet with the other. It was a bad time to find out Orri was worthless as a shield.
Tor and Olaf slashed forward while leaning into the

men covering their retreat. Luckily, the wake of bodies tripped up the Picts that were coming in from all sides.

Olaf was strong, as if this had been the first battle he'd seen that day. Unfortunately for the crowd, his natural stroke seemed to fall neck high on most Picts.

The fear of losing their heads created a barrier the front line Picts tried not to cross, but the shoving from anxious idiots in the back just teed them up for Olaf, and the heads left the shoulders, one by one.

Blood turned to mud as the bodies piled up where they'd stood.

Rage pounded in his temples, but Tor struggled to keep from giving in to the berserker inside. They'd never kill them all, so he needed to figure out other ways than the fear of Olaf to slow the onslaught down.

Orri stepped up, gripping the knife as he slashed at his countrymen. He had a warrior's heart.

"You're going to have to cut deeper than that if we're going to get out of this alive, boy!" Tor yelled.

Though not killing blows, for every cut he made with the stroke of the knife two Picts would leave the fight to drag the injured away. In some ways, Orri was clearing the field as much as Tor and Olaf.

Following the boy's lead, Tor started slashing to wound, often low. Men fell where they were, and the oncomers either dragged them out of the way or tripped over the writhing pile.

They were backing into sort of a funnel where the way was narrowest near the gate. They were almost out.

"Olaf!" Tor yelled. "Cut them in the legs."

"I prefer the necks." Olaf laughed like a boy who'd hooked his first fish.

Tor pried his hatchet from a man's shoulder, then stabbed Ice Breaker into another's hip. Two more men to add to the blue wall.

He could see the ponies and carts loaded with the

## HOW UBBI LOST HIS TONGUE

wounded Norse.

Why are they still here?

A blue face ran past, Tor jerked his stomach in, but not enough. The Picts dagger raked across his belly. "Aaagh!" It was a shallow cut, but it burned like the Christian hell.

Olaf stopped the Pict's face with his axe. "You alright?"

"No!" The Picts kept falling, but more kept coming.

"I'll see you in Valhalla!" Olaf sounded as if he was having as much fun as if he were fighting with his friends in the hall.

How was he even alive?

Tor coughed as smoke filled his lungs.

"Fire! Fire!" voices echoed on the wind.

Ubbi rode by on one of the ponies, clearing a path in the army the width of the cart it had in tow. Tor grabbed Olaf to break him from his bloodlust, and they ran behind the cart until they were outside the gate.

But Ubbi wasn't through. He turned the cart back and made another pass inside.

Nearly thrown from the cart with every Pict plowed under its wheels, Hallstein and Einar threw fiery torches at anything that would burn between sloshes of ale. Soon smoke was billowing from the stables. Fire had caught at the foot of the wall, and orange and yellow flames were painting the blue door of Drest's hall black as coal.

"Fire! Fire!" echoed throughout the town and square. The words spread as fast as the flames.

Ubbi plowed a path back through the gates and as many Northmen as could fit in the cart jumped inside. A second cart appeared with Wid wielding the reins, filled with the injured from under the witch's healing tree.

As the ponies and carts escaped into the bogs, Tor looked back to see the extent of Ubbi's distraction. The village was burning as far as he could see. That's what Ubbi had been doing while the queen made a fool of her king.

Drest may have wanted them dead, but his army of Picts weren't willing to lose their houses to the fire just to chase a handful of Vikings to the sea. Ubbi the Tongueless had lit the fires on his first raid, after all.

# UNCATCHABLE

As soon as the smoke in the air gave way to the moorish fog, Ubbi gave the reins of his cart to Einar and slipped back with the others to die in peace. Orri wasn't injured, but he looked like he was dying inside as he stared back on his old village, burning. His father had just sacrificed him to the Vikings, again.

The rain began to fall. *Great.* Ubbi pulled the priests cloak over his head.

As he did, he could hear Wid the trader speaking Pictish gibberish from the lead cart. "The rain is lucky, should help with your escape."

Was he brave or stupid? The air was as thick with resentment of Picts as it was with humidity.

Olaf, who'd been riding near the front like a man who hadn't been bloodied at all that day, shouted back. "Tor! Come up here and tell me what this trader is saying!"

Tor trotted up. "What do you need, Olaf? I've got to keep watch to the rear."

"He said the rain should help you with your escape." Orri translated.

"I guess Wid is an idiot, then, which is why he got us into this mess in the first place." Olaf rode up close to Wid and stared at him until he cowered in his seat. "Because this rain is sure to put those fires out. And when it does, we'll have the same army on our heels that he promised to help us recruit. And Drest's army won't be slowed down by carts full of dying men who won't even be able to pull an oar once we get them back in the ships." Olaf shifted his glance to the back of Wid's cart with disdain, as if he himself wasn't among the injured just two hours before. Ubbi sat up straighter.

"If there's enough rain to put out the fires, then the bogs will flood," Orri decided to explain, "As long as we make it to Scone before they do, the river will be up, the current will be fast, and your ships will be uncatchable." The waterlogged trail sucked at the wheels of the cart like an old man trying to get a piece of meat from a bowl of soup.

"*We'll* be uncatchable?" Tor raised an eyebrow. "You said you wanted to see Norway, didn't you, Orri? I think you've earned your chance."

"No, he hasn't," Olaf said.

Orri lowered his head as if he couldn't believe he'd said it out loud.

"We've got three ships and lost a lot of men." Tor rode up beside Olaf. "Even a king's son can man an oar."

Olaf gave Wid a gap-toothed grin. "How about you, Pict? Ever been to sea before?"

Ubbi tried to keep his eyes away from Orri. He'll wish he was dead if Tor or Olaf figure out it was his big mouth that got them into this mess in the first place. Ubbi recognized their surroundings. Scone was in the distance. Smoke was still rising from the ashes of the hall. The only thing left was the blackened smokestack, standing tall like a monument to lives lost for a king's ransom. Or was it for a Viking's glory? Olaf and Tor watched the village. A woman, drawing water from the well in the square, stared back as they passed. She didn't run, didn't scream. Just watched.

As Ubbi watched the watchers, he reached down and patted about his waist. Nothing. His pulse quickened. Had he lost it? He reached around his back. *There.* He was leaning on it. He pulled his wineskin around the front. It had been cut, and its contents drained. With blackened

## HOW UBBI LOST HIS TONGUE

fingers, he pinched at it until he found what he was searching for. The stone. Ubbi caught his breath.

Hallstein stared at him like he was a madman. Orri's eyes were fixed on the empty wineskin.

"Here." Hallstein offered Ubbi his wineskin which he'd dyed red.

Orri was trying to look him in the eyes. "What was that?"

Ubbi ignored his penetrating stare and took the skin from Hallstein. Why were his hands shaking? *Why should I care if I lost it, anyway?*

He could use a drink to dull the pain of his cuts, the jostling of the cart, and the grate of Orri's annoying accent.

Smells like firewater.

Hallstein smiled and nodded to goad him on. Firewater not only threatened to burn his tongue but also his soul, or so he'd heard.

Ubbi needed to rest, not go berserk.

"Go on. It'll burn, but it'll help with the healing."

The idea of letting firewater touch his tongue was almost as frightening as having it cut out in the first place. He winced as he cautiously opened his mouth. The bandages the girl with the big brown eyes plastered to the cuts on his face pulled like prying fingers, like the big man that pulled his mouth apart in Scone. He watched as the place of his torture passed from sight.

"Just ahead, men," Tor called back. "Turn the ponies loose and leave the carts. I want every able man to grab an oar."

"That means you, Hallstein," Olaf teased.

Ubbi knew he meant it.

"Split the wounded between the ships," Tor continued. "With any luck, we'll be sailing up the coast before Stingy Jack can light his lantern.

# PLEDGE TO THE JARL

The river was fast, and just as the Pict said, the moors flooded behind them. The way would be impassable for Drest's army.

As they traveled, two more men were lost, so Olaf collected the souls. As soon as they arrived at the coast, Tor had some of the able-bodied make a funeral pyre, while others loaded the ships.

As they set fire to the bodies, Olaf drank from the red flask.

"Men, we failed." Olaf gave his speech. "We came here to form an alliance and get an army. Instead, we made an enemy. All because some boys put their own personal glory ahead of my success." He scowled at Ubbi as if he was about to throw him on the pyre.

"What are you drinking, Olaf?" Tor asked.

Olaf waived him off. "We had a real chance, here. Good warriors died. And now we bring nothing but ourselves to help drive the Angles from the Southern Isles. So, I have decided to make sure that the only story that will be told about Ubbi and Orri—is that they never made it off Pictish soil." Olaf drew his sword. "Einar…give Orri your sword."

"But Ubbi did well." Einar looked confused. "He lit the fires."

"You'll get your sword back when I'm done." Olaf swung his axe down, like a practice stroke.

Olaf shook his head. "Ubbi, you messed up, but you proved you have a warrior's heart. That's why I'm letting

## HOW UBBI LOST HIS TONGUE

you die with a blade in your hand. Maybe you'll be there to greet me when I get to Valhalla, and we can laugh about all of this."

Tor thrust himself between Olaf and the boys, Icebreaker drawn. "I don't know what's gotten into you, Olaf. We need these two at the oar."

"I humored you before, Tor." Olaf circled like a shark. "You know the Pict will be worthless at sea. And Ubbi won't be whole again for months, if ever." Olaf tried to push Tor out of the way.

Tor swung Ice Breaker across, knocking Olaf's axe aside. The air filled with the ring of iron.

"We too strived for glory, Olaf. If missing the mark is your measure, then Ketill should have us both killed when we return to the Southern Isles." Tor couldn't believe he had to draw his sword again. He tasted the salt of sweat on his tongue. "If you want to be a leader then you must accept that sometimes people will let you down. These two are young. Let them learn from their mistakes."

"You make a good point, Tor. I forgot about Ketill. I almost broke his arm one time—did you know that?" Olaf smiled in a way that made the hair stand up on Tor's neck. "I can handle Ketill, but we cannot be divided."

Olaf faked left, Tor countered.

"You would fight me, over a stable boy and a Pict Prince?"

"You would fight me over them?" Tor countered again.

"All right." Olaf leaned on the handle of his axe. "Make me Jarl, and I'll let them live."

Why was his friend doing this now? In front of the men.

"I will do as you ask." Olaf wrapped his big hand behind Tor's neck and pulled him close. "Because you are my general and chief advisor, and I promise to listen to you always."

Tor glanced back at the horrified Ubbi and Orri.

"If you kill Orri, then Drest will be sure to move his

army north. Ketill can barely keep the Gaels at bay. You would risk being flanked by the Picts as well?"

"Would you?" Olaf released his grip. "Be the first to recognize me, and you will save more than these two boys. You'll be protecting all of our people in the Kingdom of the Isles."

Tor considered killing Ubbi and Orri himself.

Instead, he bowed his head. "My lord."

Olaf responded in a somber tone. "Tor, you are my general. And your sword is now my sword."

Tor could feel the blood pulsing in his temples.

"As proof of your loyalty, I want you to give me your soul."

Out of habit when feeling threatened, Tor put his hand on Ice Breaker's hilt.

Olaf raised his eyebrow and leaned forward on the axe.

*What had happened to him?* Tor moved his hand to the soul ring hanging around his neck. He'd never cared much about it before, but this made no sense. "What is this about?"

"It's a sign of unity and strength—that I'll never turn against you, and you'll never turn against me."

Tor felt a twitch in his right eye. He unsheathed Ice Breaker.

Olaf locked eyes with him, stood up straight, and raised the head of the axe off the ground.

Tor had the advantage. He could end this right now.

Tor exhaled slowly, like he was about to dive into the fjord in winter, raised Ice Breaker to his throat, and cut the worn leather thong from around his neck.

He shook his soul ring into the palm of his hand. *Ubbi and Orri would suffer at the oar for this.* "Do you think you can carry it?"

"If you give it willingly, I will. So I've been told." Olaf pulled out the red flask and emptied it down his gullet.

"Who told you that?" Tor thought about the tall

stranger in the village. The man with the staff that no one seemed to know.

"Let's find out if it's true, together, eh?"

Tor just shook his head. *I knew coming here was a bad idea.* He stared Olaf in the eyes.

"You have my sword, and my soul." He pushed his soul into Olaf's palm. Before he let it go, he thought about how proud he and Olaf were when they could finally afford to cover their filthy souls with gold. Half the men who served under them had done it since, thanks to Tor and Olaf's ambition. And for that same ambition, as many had given their souls to the grave.

Hours before, Olaf almost had too.

Tor let go of his burden, pulled his hand away, and couldn't believe Olaf was holding it in his hand.

Olaf's smile returned as he stared at it. Too big to fit on a finger, too small to fit on an arm. With a plink, Olaf dropped it into his new red flask.

As Tor watched the men line up to pay their allegiance, he felt as hollow inside as the sound the flask made every time another soul dropped inside.

"You have my sword, and my soul," Einar pledged first. *Plink!*

"My hammer, and my soul, and my firewater." *Plink!* Hallstein winked.

"Good," said Olaf. "I'm going to need it."

Ubbi and Orri were last in line to make their pledge.

"Not you two." Olaf raised his axe to stop them. "I have a sack full of souls already from the men who died because of your foolishness. I will not give you the chance to betray me again. Tor saved you today. Give your souls to him if he'll take them."

Tor waved them off. *This is ridiculous.* "I don't want your souls. These two are under my protection." Tor eyed every man and boy that was standing. Then he talked to Orri. "I will make good use of you. We need your quick mind and sharp tongue."

He turned his attention to Ubbi. "And you, Ubbi the Tongueless, have fought bravely today. You have razed two villages and avenged the deaths of your friends. You have shown us all that you are a true warrior." *Anything to lift their spirits and save their necks.*

"Enough," Olaf interrupted. "Your praise of these stable boys is making my axe thirst."

"Go." Tor was glad to send Ubbi and Orri away. "Use your wits to collect some wood for the fires." There were thirty men with their jaws open that deserved that praise more. Tor felt like he needed to bathe in the river. No one had seen a tongue bath like that since a forest cat stowed away on the ship.

# THE STONE AND THE SOUL

As Ubbi and Orri walked into the woods, they could still hear Olaf talking to the men. "This is a great day for me, and I am honored to be your Jarl. What took you so long?" The boom of his voice and the echo of the men's laughter bounced off the trees. "Together, we will make our glory. And I will make you wealthy. And someday we will come back here. I promise. We will make things right."

Orri spoke, "When we return, I will need you to help me free my mother."

Ubbi didn't think Orri understood what making things right meant. He also realized he would probably have to get used to Orri's terrible Pict accent. As they were Tor's men now, they'd probably be spending a lot of time together.

Nothing had gone Ubbi's way on this trip. He'd lost his friends and his chance at glory. And he couldn't even complain about it. *I'll never be heard again.*

"Don't look so upset." Orri didn't seem as distraught about this arrangement as he should've been. "Being the general's only men could have its advantages. He'll probably keep us very close. And since you can't talk, I bet he tells you everything."

Orri was already scheming. He could probably talk the ears off a rock.

"We may have just traded glory for power, eh? You do still have the stone, don't you?"

Ubbi picked up a stick and broke it in two against a

tree, trying to pretend he didn't hear.

*Should've been Orri's head. That'd be the end of it.*

"Come on, I won't tell. As long as we can try it."

*When had he seen?*

"At first I didn't know what you were up to, but I was glad you kept it after the queen turned me out."

*Your father didn't exactly fight it, either.*

"She's the one that talked my father into trading the stone for the army. Everything came at a price with that woman." Orri cracked a piece of pine across his knee. "My father didn't need any reason to help drive the Angles out of the Isles. Better to have the Vikings ally with him than with Mac Alpin, is what he'd always say."

*I guess this trip didn't work out for any of us then.* Ubbi thought about that stone. He was curious. *Of course, he was curious.* It'd been on his mind ever since the escape. And now that Olaf had it out for him, what did he have to lose?

"May only work on Pict soil, for all I know."

Ubbi fished an empty wineskin around his belt. He was surprised how comfortable the priest's robe was. *Maybe the Picts were onto something with their skirts, after all.* He'd never tell.

He looked over his shoulder, then back. They were alone. He cut the wineskin from his belt and saw it had a hole in it. He ran his thumb across a matching one in the robe just near his hip. *That one could've done me in, right there.*

Ubbi put the tip of his seax through the hole in the ruined skin and opened it up. He thought about how easily he could've been one of the bodies they burned that day.

*Would Olaf have taken my soul had I died in Scone, or left it for the ravens?*

"That's it," Orri urged him on. "Let's see it."

Ubbi pinched the stone out into the palm of his hand, then pulled it close. *No reason to trust Orri not to grab it.*

## HOW UBBI LOST HIS TONGUE

*Barely know him, really.*

"That's it? Are you sure?" Apparently Orri didn't trust him either.

*Only one way to find out.* Ubbi fished out his soul ring and pulled its leather necklace up and over his head. He hadn't undone that worn leather knot since his soul was cut from his chest three years earlier. Ubbi struggled to untie it.

"Let me." Orri snatched Ubbi's soul and was instantly dragged to the ground under the weight of it.

Idiot.

Orri left the ring on the ground, not that he had a choice, and climbed back to his feet, "I guess you'll have to do it."

The cuts on Ubbi's cheeks burned from smiling. *Don't laugh.* Ubbi exhaled slowly. *Laughing would be torture.* He froze until the feeling passed, picked his soul up off the ground, and cut the knot, loosing his soul from its tether.

Orri leaned in.

Ubbi turned a little as he dropped the stone into the ring, took a deep breath and stared at it. *What is this going to do to me?* Ubbi looked to Orri for guidance, or confidence…something.

Orri shrugged. "Maybe if I hold on to you it'll work for both of us."

*Or neither of us.* Ubbi grabbed Orri's hand and put it on his shoulder. Before the Pict could say another word, Ubbi went right to his ring, lifted it up, and let the stone pass through.

The world seemed to shift, but nothing changed. Or maybe Ubbi just blinked. *Stupid Picts.* He shoved Orri's hand off his shoulder, retied his soul ring around his neck, picked up his pile of wood, and made his way back to the ship.

"Ubbi, wait." Orri scrounged around for wood, but Ubbi just stomped away. *My friends died for this?*

*Superstitious bog folk.*

When Ubbi broke out of the wood line, he dropped his sticks. *What in the Christian hell?*

Orri ran up beside him. "Ubbi, wait, don't tell...Where'd they go?" He spun on his heels. "They left us."

They were gone. No ships. No men. No evidence of the camp at all. Not even the black remnants of the campfires.

"The only thing they left was the funeral pyre," Orri said, scratching his head.

Still smoking.

"I guess we can go back to my father's." Orri stared out to vacant sea.

*That'll work out well for you...maybe.*

There was something wrong—besides the fact that Ubbi'd been abandoned to die at the hand of the Picts. They hadn't been in the woods that long. Not enough for the ships to be completely out of sight.

Ubbi fixed his gaze on the horizon. The sea was smooth as glass.

"Come on, I'll make peace with my father." Orri tugged Ubbi's robe. "Maybe he'll think you're a priest." Orri tried to look upbeat. "If we're lucky, we'll get back in time for dinner."

Ubbi ambled along behind. What choice did he have but to throw himself on the mercy of the Pict King? His stomach roiled at the thought of his situation. As they passed the field where Ubbi'd watched the ponies, they were gone too. No shelter, no nothing.

"You Vikings are thorough." Orri shook his head. "I was hoping to ride back. You don't put horses on the ships, do you?"

Ubbi shook his head. They didn't this time. Nothing made sense. He knew for a fact there was a trail before, right over there.

"At least it had stopped raining." Orri's babbling was as

relentless as the flow of the river.

A parliament of white owls and a murder of crows lifted into the air at their coming, like Ubbi and Orri had interrupted a council of the birds.

What an odd country.

Ubbi skipped a stone across the water. Ahead, he noticed smoke rising from an island upstream.

"Move faster." Orri increased his pace.

Ubbi wasn't in a hurry to march back into the enemy's camp. One he'd set fire to just hours before. He saw a glimmer underfoot and reached down to pick it up. He had to figure out a way home. As he straightened his back, his finger slipped through... *A soul!* Ubbi threw it to the ground.

Orri hustled back. "We've got to get out of here. Somebody took the bodies." He jerked Ubbi forward. "Don't you remember, or were you asleep?"

Ubbi had no idea what Orri was talking about.

"Olaf wouldn't stop talking about it when we passed. This is where they fought the men of Scone. There were Pict bodies everywhere when we passed before."

Ubbi shrugged him off and stared at the road. Iron plated soul rings glinted in the fading sun. A chill gripped Ubbi's spine. He reached down and picked up another soul ring. *Impossible.* He'd never picked up a man's soul ring before. The only way it could be done is if they gave it to you or if they were dead. *Who takes the body but leaves the soul?*

Ubbi felt something move underfoot.

"Come on!" Orri's cheeks were red and sweaty. "There's something evil in this place."

Ubbi saw movement, but there was nothing there. Just earth and rings. The road ahead was covered with them.

They passed the source of the smoke. Another funeral pyre. This one built on an island in the river.

"That's where Tor had them burn the bodies of the

Vikings that they'd lost. What the—?" Orri pushed Ubbi aside, sending him down to the ground.

Ubbi reached for Orri's ankle to trip the fool up, but he was too quick, hopping off the trail like a scared rabbit.

Something slithered up Ubbi's ankle. Instincts took over, and he kicked and pulled away.

Like a slithering snake, a vine sprouted from the earth to take hold of his leg.

They were coming up everywhere.

Death blue and slightly glowing, the vines sprouted through the center of the vacant souls, as if the rings were some witch's seed.

One moved under Ubbi's elbow. "Gnnh!" he grunted. Thorns cut through the thick robe and scraped at his skin. Like needles of burning fire.

"Ubbi! Give me your hand." Orri was just out of reach.

*Come closer, fool!* If Ubbi'd had a rock, he'd have thrown it at him.

Behind Orri, from deep in the forest, came a horrible howl. Orri neglected Ubbi for what may come.

Ubbi freed his sword from its sheath, and with a downward snap, cut the vine from its seed. Its thorns still clung to his arm like a tentacle of fire, and red sap bled from the pruning. The smell was putrid sweet.

A low vibration rumbled out of the forest, but Ubbi was too busy weeding the garden to worry about that. Yet.

Ubbi hacked down at the vine slithering up his leg. Just before he made the cut, he could've sworn it coiled itself into a hand to tighten its grip around his thigh. As soon as he separated it from its soul, the weed fell to the ground in a pile.

Ubbi pushed himself to his feet and hopped over the burgeoning crop of evil weeds to escape to the forest's edge. He'd have cursed if he still had his tongue. Instead he punched Orri hard for abandoning him.

Orri stood as still as stone. Didn't flinch, didn't

## HOW UBBI LOST HIS TONGUE

complain.

Ubbi followed the path of Orri's eyes and almost dropped his sword.

Not six paces away, they faced what looked like a giant Forest cat perched high on a fallen tree. It was black as a midnight shadow, except for a single white dot on its breast and two glowing, yellow eyes.

The cat raised its great paw from the corpse of a large, gray wolf and licked red blood from between its toes.

Ubbi slowly raised his sword. *What kind of nightmare is that?* He'd never heard of lions in Pictavia, and there was nothing like that thing in all of Norway. Except maybe the bears.

Ubbi felt a vine prodding at his heel but dared not shift the attention of his blade.

"Take out the stone." Orri breathed the words out, barely moving his lips.

Without turning their heads, Ubbi and Orri locked eyes.

"The stone." Orri had sweat dripping down his cheek. "Drop the stone through your soul again." Orri eased his hand to Ubbi's robe. As Ubbi felt his grip lock down, the cat raised its head, and the body of the wolf fell to the ground with a thud.

The sun was setting, and the fog was rolling in from the moors.

*What I wouldn't give for a torch.*

Deep in the forest, Ubbi heard whistling.

First the cat, then Ubbi and Orri all turned to see.

A man was skipping down along a forest path, just their direction. He was holding a bag at his side in one hand and a lantern made from a turnip in the other. The light from the lantern glowed hot and red and bright enough to cast shadows.

Orri jerked Ubbi close. "Use the stone!" His eyes were wide and wild.

The thorns on the vine clawed at the back of Ubbi's

thigh.

As Ubbi searched his pocket, he turned to see the garden had matured. The phosphorescent vines were coiling into the shapes of men, like dead warriors clawing their way out of the soil.

Ubbi found the stone and clasped it tight in his shaking hand.

The cat dropped from its perch to the ground and stared at Ubbi with its bright, yellow eyes. Bark flew as it dragged its finger length claws across the tree.

Ubbi threw up his sword, but lost his grip on the stone. It hit his foot, then bounced into the leaves.

Orri scrambled down to find it, drawing the attention of the cat. The beast's hiss was like a rogue storm, fouling the air with the scent of death.

The whistling man had gotten so close the red light from his lantern reflected off Ubbi's quaking blade, sending its light dancing along the forest floor.

This red distraction caught the attention of the cat, and it pounced, its tail knocking Orri into Ubbi's feet. The vines tripped Ubbi up, and they both went barreling to their backs, like two helpless turtles, caught in a sea of vines.

Ubbi's head hit something hard. When he regained focus, his head was swimming and burned like fire.

A vine had tied Ubbi's sword hand down, so he brought his other to the pain. There was blood.

What felt like greedy hands raked their talons over Ubbi's chest and legs, pinning the rest of him to the ground.

Ubbi felt lost.

The slice of a moon was already high overhead, and Ubbi could see the first star. Orri was beside him but had gotten to his knees.

"Grab onto me, you fool!" Orri grabbed Ubbi's hand away from his head and trapped it against his coat. Ubbi clamped down with everything he had and tried to pull

## HOW UBBI LOST HIS TONGUE

himself up. *No use.* He could feel the thorns piercing the length of his legs.

"Hang on!" Orri pulled his own soul ring from around his neck, dropped the stone in, and jerked the ring up.

# THE RETURNING

Orri's lips were moving like he was saying a prayer. Ubbi let go of his sword, pulled himself up using Orri's coat, then released his grip. They were sitting in the road, surrounded by bodies. Pictish warriors.

Ubbi gently raised his hand to the burning spot on his head. "Gnnh!" he growled. He pulled his hand back and saw blood on his fingertips, and the soul ring still dangling in his palm.

It was raining again.

The sound of running water burbled down the river, and the bugs sang their evening songs from the forest. The sky had gotten darker, and the fog thicker.

Ubbi scanned the forest edge, but there was no sign of the yellow eyes of the giant black cat or the whistling man with the turnip lantern and the sack.

Orri's jaw loosed as he pointed toward a ghostly red glow, hovering over bodies as it passed.

Ubbi watched as a following of small, white whisps of light bounced along behind and followed it into the moors.

Ubbi grabbed Orri's still pointing hand, pulled open his tight grip, and emptied it of the stone.

Whether of David or of Scone, Ubbi took it back and hid it deep in his pocket. He and Orri helped each other to their feet and put their soul rings back around their necks.

There was a yellow glow in the distance, coming from the direction of the ships. For once, Orri kept his mouth shut while they walked back toward the sea. There, where

# HOW UBBI LOST HIS TONGUE

they'd left them, was the Viking camp.

Tor stood up from one of many fires and walked toward them to meet them along the road.

"Where have you boys, been? I was worried you'd done something stupid."

Ubbi looked at Orri, the only one who could ever explain it. "We got lost."

Tor looked at them with a raised brow. "I'm glad you made it back. I gave up my soul for you two. You owe me." Tor looked at them like a farmer who'd just found his lost sheep. "Because of the storm, we decided not to leave until dawn." Tor smiled and put his hand on Ubbi's shoulder. "What's this?" Thorns tugged at the priestly robe as Tor freed the prickly piece of vine.

He sniffed at it. "Is this blood weed?"

Ubbi shrugged. His eyes fixed on the vine to make sure it didn't move.

"Never seen it this fresh before."

Ubbi rubbed the sickly-sweet aroma from his nostrils.

"We found it in the woods...while we were lost." Orri lied. "Ubbi thought some of your crew might be able to make firewater out of it."

"He thought that, did he?" Tor stared at Ubbi, as if he could confess.

Ubbi stared back, then plucked a thorn out of his sleeve.

Orri turned to look over his shoulder, back down the road from where they'd come.

Tor's eyes followed his gaze. "I'll get this to Einar and Hallstein. Do you think you can find more?" Tor held the vine like a dead snake.

Ubbi tried to keep calm, but he found himself shaking his head like a child being asked to go outside by himself in the dark.

"No," Orri said in a dead calm. "We were far gone. I wouldn't feel safe trying to get there again."

Tor stared into the woods. "Too bad. If you could figure

out a way to keep Olaf in firewater, you might get back in his good graces. But for now, this'll do." Tor stared at the blood weed.

Ubbi knew Tor had never seen fresh blood weed before. *Nobody had.*

"You two have lost a lot, and you look like you could use some sleep. Get some rest, Ubbi. I'll have someone else stand guard for us tonight."

# HAVE YOU READ VIKING LOST?

If you liked the story of Ubbi the Tongueless, continue the adventure by catching up with Tor's life, twenty years later, when he gets an unexpected visit from Ubbi and Orri in a storm-wrecked Viking ship.

## Full of Norse history, magic, and fighting vikings! I love it!

**The Vikings want the village. The gods want the souls. Can Tor save his family before everything goes to Hella?**

Read on to find out more…

# VIKING LOST

With one son preparing for marriage, the other about to have his soul ring painfully cut from his chest, things were finally looking up for Tor and his family. He was even thinking of ways to fix his own marriage with the boys' stepmother. But when a weather-worn dragon ship washed into his hidden fjord with a half-dead Viking giant, a Christian slave girl, and members of Tor's old crew, the life he'd made began to unravel.

Once, Tor had traded his own cracked and mottled soul for glory — he wanted better for his sons. But even they could be lured by the Viking's promises of adventure and riches, compared to their life of want and runaway goats. Only Tor knows that if he can't defeat the giant, he and his family might be the village's first sacrifice to the gods he left behind.

Viking Lost is the first novel in the exciting Saga of Souls historical fantasy series.

**If you like Norse Mythology, soul-less Vikings, and want a glimpse of the underworld, read Viking Lost!**

Available from your favorite bookseller's website.

# ABOUT THE AUTHOR

Derek Nelsen is the author of the Saga of Souls series. As a Norske American he is fascinated by the myths and folklore of his Scandinavian ancestors, and of course, the Vikings.

He lives in the Blue Ridge Mountains of Western North Carolina with his beautiful wife, Lisa, and their three wonderful children—far from Hel and safe from draugr, which is more than he can say for his characters.

Track Derek's progress, help shape the story, and get some free stuff by signing up at **www.dereknelsen.com**.

*For readers who know trolls don't just live on the internet.*

*For more information:*
www.dereknelsen.com
derek@dereknelsen.com

Milton Keynes UK
Ingram Content Group UK Ltd.
UKHW041318241024
2361UKWH00041B/402